The Regulars
Tales from a Suffolk pub

Written & Illustrated by

GARY STOCKER

Stories by Gary & Paul Stocker

Copyright © 2020 Gary Stocker

All rights reserved.

ISBN: 1495488504
ISBN-13: 978-1495488504

DEDICATION

To the late Jim Sanders, former landlord of the King's Head establishment, Mendlesham, who taught us how to drink. To Paul Allen, the present landlord, who lets us continue with our teachings.

CONTENTS

	Acknowledgements	i
1	Introducing the 'Lazy Dog'	1
2	The Face	5
3	Bed, Breakfast & Beer	53
4	The Snobs	88
5	The Dark Lord rises	126
6	A Large, Stiff One	170
7	A Wedding and a Wake	208
8	Mistletoe and Crime	252

ACKNOWLEDGEMENTS

My brother Paul, without whom, this book would not exist. My mother Linda, whose creative genes allowed me to create this book.

INTRODUCING
THE LAZY DOG

Welcome to the 'Lazy Dog' public house! It is slightly run down and in need of a lick of paint, although not without a certain charm. The pub is situated in the gentle village of Sandwich Green in the heart of the Suffolk countryside. Population: 346. Village idiots: 7.

The Regulars

The pub was owned by the brewery but has been operated for the last eighteen months by two brothers; Harry and Jeff Knocker. Harry was the smarter of the pair, although being the eldest sibling does not necessarily go hand in hand with being the wisest. There always seems to be something missing in Harry's life. When he was installed as the Landlord, he somehow got the brewery to change the name of the pub from 'The Windmill' to the 'Lazy Dog,' allegedly after his ex-wife.

Jeff was the pub chef and chief hanger-on. He intentionally remains in his brother's shadow, through laziness and lack of desire. Harry tolerates him as they are both aware of their E-status within the Knocker ecosystem. The brothers are ably assisted by a talkative Bristolian barmaid, Julie, very economic with her workload but less so with her vocabulary. Her focus in life appears to be speaking glossily about her better half,

The Lazy Dog

Paul. It could be said she slightly exaggerates his escapades, but then again it could also be said that it was just plain bullshit.

The final piece of the Lazy Dog workforce is an elderly lady known as 'Cobweb' Mary. She is employed on a part time basis as the cleaner. Mary was proud of her work at the pub, as was Harry. Jeff has other ideas. Harry spotted Mary rearranging the baked beans on the shelf at the local shop. He thought the fact that she turned all the labels to the front meant she had a cleaning fetish. The reality was she was just hiding the sell buy dates.

The pub itself is a 16th century erection that has survived a few wars, namely One, Two and the landlord war between the local rival the Rat's Head. It has sustained substantial cosmetic damage, such as the time in 1943 when a German Bomber landed on the roof. To this day

The Regulars

there are still rumours of a ghostly airman in the attic, who appears infrequently to put the wind up the publican of the time.

THE FACE

It was a misty Suffolk morning in Sandwich Green. Whirls of thick, white fog hung in the early morning air around the establishment of The Lazy Dog. The pub gave off an eerie silence and a faint glow from inside illuminated Mrs

The Regulars

Goodrum's cat, cleaning itself on the window ledge. Inside the pub, the main bar was a picture of stillness, except for the faint smog of the after-hours cigarette smokers. The place was literally littered with corpses. Drunken, hungover corpses, strewn around the chairs, tables and in one case, in the unused fireplace. Someone gave out a cough to let the others know that the air was still breathable, barely. It was just loud enough to stir Harry Knocker, the landlord, himself perched upon a stool behind the bar with his head resting on a packet of nuts. Harry forced his eyes open to witness the carnage that lay before him. A glance at his watch informed him that it was seven thirty-three A.M.

'Christ! The pub opens again in three hours; all this lot will be back in again then,' but first, they have to leave!

'Right, you horrible lot - wake up! Out you go before I charge you a night's bed and breakfast!' implored Harry. One waif began to stir, slowly rising and taking in a lungful of stale tobacco air.

'Blimey, Harry. What time is it?' called out a bald sixty-year-old man who should have known better.

'Half seven, Baz.'

'Bloody hell, Maureen'll go mental!'

'I wouldn't worry yourself too much, Baz. She's over there, next to the plant pot.'

Barry glared through the mist and, yes, his fiancée had passed out next to the half-dead spider plant. Baz was one of the pub regulars. Along with his ageing squeeze, Maureen, they were seen as two of the more sensible clientele by the two brothers. The only thing that let Barry down was his attire. He insisted on wearing a pair of joggers and a vest, which wouldn't have been so bad if the hair on his body wasn't making up for the lack of it on his head.

'Think you better give her the kiss of life, Baz!' Harry advised. 'Now, is my dopey little brother in here, still?' Harry spotted the off-white chef's trousers leaning against the bottom of the bar. He poured out a drop of lemonade and chucked it over Jeff… nothing! Harry then poured out a half of lager and repeated the process. Same negative result. Harry then decided to pull one of the more unsavoury of the regulars, Brassie, from under his stool and leant him up against Jeff's face.

'Wait for it...' Sure enough, Jeff 's nose started twitching and one eye opened. A dawn of realisation came over his face and then he bolted upright, pushing Brassie back over.

'I hope I haven't slept like that all night?' Jeff stated hastily.

'Sorry, bro. You looked like you were enjoying your cuddles, so I left you like it' Harry cried, inwardly creasing.

'You git,' responded Jeff, looking round, 'How many are left in here?'

'Only Baz, Maureen, Brassie and big Cliff.'

'Cliff? He was driving!'

The Face

Harry pulled a set of keys from behind the bar, 'Don't worry, I took his keys off him when he got to his eighth pint.'

'Hey, that's his new Merc!'

'That's why I look after him,' Harry winked. 'He's six foot six and as wide, look at him over there. We wouldn't need a dining room table to put your dodgy old food on. He takes up the room. Literally!'

Suddenly there was the disgusting sound of someone clearing a load of phlegm from their throat. Jeff and Harry stared at each other blankly.

'I thought you said it was just Baz, Maureen, Brassie and Cliff?' Jeff asked as he wiped some leftovers from his collar.

Harry glanced round nervously, 'I thought so too?'

The disgusting sound was heard again and then Father Gorn popped up from behind the bar.

'Aah Father, I'd forgotten you were in last night.' Harry said with faint recollection.

The Regulars

Father Gorn was the Sandwich Green vicar and partial to a tipple or three. He had piercing blue eyes set behind a pair of granny glasses and bright, curly, orange hair. His striking physog was completed by a nose redder than a certain reindeer at a certain time of year.

'Bless you Harry, you've made an old vicar very happy, sir,' quipped the holy man.

'Oh really?'

'It was nice of you to find a space for the church fund raising committee.'

Harry looked surprised. 'There was only you, Father.'

'Thank you, my boy, thank you,' Father Gorn started surveying the place, 'I'm sure I've left my bell ringer in here somewhere?'

'No, I wouldn't think so, Father,' Harry replied, 'Too big to fit in here.'

Father Gorn looked back to where he emerged, 'Found it!'

He then proceeded to pull up a seventy-year old lady with poor eyesight. 'Edna,

The Face

dear. Time, we got you home!'

Father Gorn turned to Harry, 'Aah, Harry, this is Edna, my new bell ringer - I wore the other one out!'

Harry and Jeff watched in disbelief.

'I bet you did!' remarked Jeff.

'Ta-ra both.' Father Gorn headed towards the front door.

'Oh Father, you better leave through the back door. I mean, we don't want to cause any unnecessary noise to our neighbours, do we?'

Father Gorn and Edna scuttled off out the back as quick as they had appeared.

Harry looked at his watch again. He had wasted far too much time now and was immediately irritated.

'Right ladies and gents, time to GO!' Just as the last word left his mouth a loud knock on the front door sent shivers down his spine. A knock on the front door at this hour spelt trouble. The previous night had been busy but nothing out of the ordinary had happened. Had it? Harry took another look around and pulled Brassie back upright. There, was this it? Scrawled across Brassies forehead in permanent marker was the word 'COCK.'

The knock on the heavy oak door was heard again.

'Quick, you lot. Get out the back!'

'What about Brassie? You'll never shift him like that.' Jeff pointed out.

'Give me those tea towels,' Harry responded, 'I'll sort it,' and then proceeded to throw them over the prone customer. 'Go and open the damn door before it wakes the whole of Sandwich Green!'

The creaky back door of the Lazy Dog opened tentatively. Harry's sunken eyes poked round the door.

'Morning Publican.'

'Officer Russell! You're about this morning.' Harry said nervously.

'Had to be. Had a few complaints you see.'

'You'd better come in, sir.'

PC Russell was not your typical village

bobby, he looked like an American city cop with his aviator shades and stubble. They didn't really go with the English bobby's uniform, but it gave Russell a bit more confidence since he lost an eye in an unfortunate dart incident at the pub in the first month of Harry and Jeff's residency.

'So... I've had reports of raucous behaviour and lots of swearing after hours.'

'Officer Russell, your mother lives next door to the pub!' responded Harry.

'All the more reason to behave... what's that smell?'

'Smell, Officer?' Harry looked round vaguely as if oblivious to the stench.

'Oh, you mean that... vomit,' Harry remarked, pointing to the pile of tea towels hiding Brassie, 'One of our patrons did not distinguish themselves very well in the middle of our main bar, we'll have it sorted in a minute!'

'That's foul! Did you not think of cleaning it up before?'

The Regulars

Jeff interjected, 'We've got a new cleaner; Harry said she could do it in the morning.'

Harry was aghast, 'I certainly did not, I gave you the job!'

Officer Russell now lost patience. 'I don't care who cleans it up. Get it moved asap!'

Harry decided to straighten things out. 'Okay Officer, we'll do it right away. Was there anything else we can do for you? Quick one for the road perhaps?'

Officer Russell lowered his shades revealing his one good eye and one false eye. It rolled in the socket as he talked.

'Mr Knocker. I vowed never to set foot in here after my accident. Since you've been looking after the place this is my third visit. See there are no more.' With that, Officer Russell turned and flicked the match he was chewing on to the bar stacked full of empties and departed.

Harry and Jeff threw a glance of relief at each other.

'Phew, that was the closest one yet!'

The Face

Jeff stated anxiously.

'We'll get caught serving after hours soon.'

'Well, we're getting away with it now. It's the only way we get some decent money in' Harry replied, wiping his forehead.

'Brassie don't half honk. He must be the smelliest man in the world after a skinful?'

'You haven't met Billy of the Ocean yet, then?' Harry then explained to Jeff all about Billy and his odour problem. Billy was a local homeless alcoholic waif, who trundled between the local villages. His favourite nesting place was the bench in front of the hedge outside the church. This was a well-chosen spot as it was about half a can drinking from the pub and the waste bin was on the small side, so Billy was usually able to pick up an odd half can of cider or the like. Unfortunately, discarded cans of deodorant are very few and far between.

Brassie eventually stirred and from

The Regulars

beneath the soiled tea cloths, a nose, mouth and eyes emerged.

'Where did she go?' coughed Brassie with the strength of ten beers on his breath.

'You mean that lady you were chatting too last night?'

'Yeah.'

'Well, you seemed to be well in for a bit,' Harry explained, 'and then you fell asleep on her.'

'Damn! That always happens.'

'Try drinking less!' said Jeff. Harry gave Jeff the dubious eye.

'It's not the drink, Brassie. You need to work on your banter. Oh, and change your T-Shirt and maybe a bath wouldn't go amiss?'

Brassie stood up, staggered to his left and put his hand in a plate of sandwiches to steady himself.

Harry continued, 'You were doing fine until you bet her you could down a pint of "Black Russian."'

'Easy.' replied Brassie.

The Face

'Yes, but your bet was to get her in the sack, and you fell asleep while halfway through the pint!' Harry exclaimed.

A lightbulb lit up above Jeff's head. 'Oh, so that's who wrote coc...' Harry cut him off sharply before he finished.

'Come on, Brassie. Let's see you out of here, now. We'll be seeing you shortly anyway I expect?'

'Yup, 11 A.M. as normal.'

Harry pointed Brassie towards the door.

'Yes, I thought so.'

Brassie exited awkwardly at the second attempt!

'Say, Harry, why does Brassie always wear the same T-shirt?' asked Jeff as the door closed.

'Oh, he's got a picture of his hero - Roger Stork, the Town football player on it.'

'That picture must be from the 70's. Did you see the moustache and sideburns?'

'It wouldn't surprise me if the T-shirt wasn't from the 70's, Jeff.'

Harry surveyed the main bar once

more. The place was its usual mess. Broken glasses, uneaten sandwiches, with the obligatory cigarette ends placed inside.

'Do you know what today is, Jeff?'

'Saturday, H.'

'True, but it's also the quarterly brewery inspection today.'

Jeff then started to take an interest in the debris. The boys only just got through the last inspection, but this time, well, they'd had it. Harry put his hands over his head and let out a squeak of frustration. Jeff placed an arm round him that lacked comfort, 'Don't worry, Harry. Your new cleaner will be here in a minute. If she's as good as you say, then she will soon sort this place out.' Harry released his head and grabbed Jeff's arm and returned it to his side.

'I feel like I run this place on my own! I wish you'd help a bit more. Your menu needs a good rehash. We've hardly taken any food orders recently.'

'Actually, I have decided on some new

The Face

dishes.'

'Go on then, surprise me.' Harry responded rather unexcitedly.

'Well, I've decided to add goulash to the menu'

'Goulash? And for what reason?'

'Dunno, just think it sounds funny.'

'Dear God!'

The main door creaked open tentatively and in walked an elderly lady of about eighty, resplendent with a blue rinse. This was Cobweb Mary; the cleaner. Under her right arm was a can of polish and there was a cloth in her left hand. She was wearing a pinny from the nineteen-fifties. She didn't look directly at the two brothers as she shimmied over to the bar. She placed the polish on an area that didn't have spilled beer on.

'Mary, you're here! Thank god. As you can see there's quite a bit to do.' Harry said suppressing his chuckle. 'Right, come on Jeff. We've got to tidy up. Someone's got to look after this place after you lot have been in here. You don't think it clears itself up do you? I'm in need of a shower and I suggest you have one too!'

Harry turned back to Cobweb Mary 'It's all yours Mary…' and then both he and Jeff sauntered out of the door.

Cobweb Mary glared at the mess for a bit and then silently pulled out a black bin liner. Holding it open at one end of a table, she then placed her feather duster on the other side and slid everything into the black bag, empty glasses, full glasses, the lot!

There was a big rug in the middle of the main bar floor that had seen better days. Mary lifted one side of this and brushed the dust, dirt and broken glass under it. She then opened another bin liner at one end of the bar and proceeded to perform the same motion with her feather duster as she did before and slid everything that was there into the black bag. Unfortunately, a whole tray of new peanuts slid in also.

Harry and Jeff re-entered the main bar.

The Face

Harry had obviously showered and changed but Jeff was exactly as he was.

'Well done, Mary. It looks a lot better. I'd better give you your wages now, then.'

Mary gave Harry an appreciative look back.

'A well-earned twenty quid. You can buy yourself a new purple rinse now.' Harry said, pulling a twenty from his wallet.

Mary nodded back in agreement and scuttled out of the main door. Harry had followed her out as far as the inner door. As he stepped on the rug, he felt the crunch of the broken glass underneath it. Jeff tittered as Harry looked down and shook his head.

'You get what you pay for, Harry.'

'Thought you were getting in the shower?' Harry snapped back.

'Well, no. Did my pits and crack though.' replied Jeff.

'Charming. Still, place is a lot better now Mary's been. Have you sorted the

The Regulars

kitchen out ready for the brewery inspection?'

'Yeah, I did it yesterday'

'But you've cooked since!'

Jeff took a moment for this to sink in, 'Oh yeah. Don't worry, I'll get on it in a minute.'

Harry walked away to the till muttering, 'Lazy sod. Good job I got the brains in the family or we'd be buggered.'

He opened the till and then any colour he had left in his face drained away.

'What's up? Profit down again?' enquired Jeff.

'Profit? We haven't seen any profit for three months! I wish you'd help a bit. You call yourself my business partner but muggins here, does all the work to get the punters in.'

Jeff stood up straight, 'I organised the quiz for the OAP's the other week!'

Harry shut the till up and turned back to Jeff, 'And what a disaster that was. We paid out more in false teeth and Zimmer repairs than we sold beer. What we need

The Face

is some big event, pack the place out. I suppose I'll have to sort that out too.'

Jeff felt this was a challenge he could rise to, 'No, No. I can do it. Give me a bit of time to come up with something. I won't let you down, bruv. I promise. It'll be the biggest event yet!'

Harry was heartened by the words but still disbelieving. 'Well, while you're thinking, can we have a look at that outside paint job before the brewery man turns up. I'm sure that old pub name is starting to show through again.'

'I can sort that out for you,' responded Jeff, sensing an improvement opportunity in Harry's eyes, 'I did a bit of decorating in my youth.'

'Yes, I remember. Redecorating the pavement, normally!'

Harry and Jeff stood outside the pub in the late morning sunshine staring up at the 'Lazy Dog' hand painted monogram. Sure, enough the previous title 'The Windmill' was becoming evident once more under the wash. A despondent Harry turned to Jeff, 'Can you really sort that?'

'What time's the inspection?'

'One o'clock.'

'What time's it now?'

'Eleven.'

Jeff looked back up at the job, 'Piece of cake.'

'Yes, but I've tried your cake!'

Just then, Jeff's normal bemused grin turned into the widest smile you've ever seen. 'I've got an idea!'

Harry's eyes narrowed, 'Oh, God.'

'No. Hear me out. We need an event, right? To get the punters in so the brewery doesn't chuck us out.'

'Yes,' replied Harry extremely nervously.

'Then we need an attraction, don't we?'

Harry knew this was too good to be true, 'Obviously. But what is there around here? The Germans flew over Suffolk every day, loaded with bombs and never bothered. Waste of a good bomb!'

'Back in a minute,' rasped Jeff, 'I've just got a few calls to make,' and with that bolted back round towards the back of the pub.

Harry called after him, 'Hurry up, we haven't got long…' as Jeff's heels disappeared around the corner.

Harry looked back up at the sign with a sense of resignation when a repetitive squeak entered his eardrum. He glanced back at the road and spotted Father Gorn and Edna pummelling up the hill on a tandem.

'Morning. Nice to see you've both recovered.'

Father Gorn slowed up, 'Doing up the place, Harry?'

'Just a bit of a spruce, Reverend. On your rounds?'

'Yes, just on my way to see Mrs Allcock. She's still a bit grief stricken after losing her husband,' the holy man replied.

'She lost him twenty-five years ago,

The Regulars

Father!'

'Yes, but I like to do my bit. Cheerio.' The tandem had just made the brow of the hill and was now gathering pace as it started to descend downhill. 'Come on, Edna. Try harder. My ankles are playing up and this seat feels like I'm sitting on a nineteenth century bobby's helmet!'

Harry watched the pair as they tailed off into the distance. 'Allcock? I bet she does.' At this point Jeff reappeared from around the corner with the same glowing smile. 'Am I a genius or am I a genius?'

'A word I do not normally associate with you,' Harry stated sarcastically, 'What have you done?'

'Sorted the event out,' replied Jeff holding a pad and a pen, 'It's gonna be big.'

'What's going on then?'

'Not what... but who!'

'Who, then?'

'Only the biggest living legend that Suffolk has ever seen,' beamed Jeff, 'Premier League footballer…

The Face

International Film Star…'

Harry was none the wiser.

'Only Roger bloody Stork, that's who.'

'Roger?' Harry was obviously not up with football.

'Stork. You know… Storky. Town football legend. He does these after dinner gigs these days cos his knee's playing up.'

Harry was impressed with his younger brother's initiative. 'How the hell did you get him, then?'

'My old mate was in the game and he owes me one, so we got him.'

'Well you do surprise me. Er. How much will it cost?' Harry replied getting back to the business end.

'He's not cheap, I grant you. But it will bring in all the footy fans.'

Harry pondered a moment, 'Sounds ideal. When can we get him?'

Jeff's smile lowered a little, 'That's the snag. He's had a cancellation, so it's got to be tonight.'

'Jeff! I can't promote this thing in six

The Regulars

days, let alone six hours!'

Jeff's smile returned, 'Don't worry about that. Brassie's a mad fan of his. I've let him know. Word will get around in no time.'

Harry put an arm around Jeff, 'I appreciate your help, brother, I really do. But this was putting us up against it somewhat.'

Jeff removed Harry's appendage, 'Trust me. It'll be cool. Right, I'm off to get some paint and I'll sort your sign out.'

* * * *

The rear car park of the 'Lazy Dog' was relatively large compared to the size of the pub. However, this expanse came in handy for the lunchtime visits of the farmers and their somewhat larger vehicles, tractors and suchlike. Once, even a combine harvester was seen parked to the rear. Although Harry had to ban it when it took out half the fence, the original pub sign and the next-door

The Face

neighbour's dog on its exit.

Jeff walked up to his clapped-out white Astra van and discovered his automobile had a flat tyre. Literally deflated he leant back on the car next to it, big Cliff's new Merc. He had a lightbulb moment and nipped back into the pub main bar to retrieve the keys for said vehicle.

The Suffolk country lanes are wide enough for the size of twenty first century cars, but God forbid if a tractor was ever coming the other way. The verge takes a bit of a beating. Jeff was poodling along a single-track road in the Mercedes with heavy metal music blaring out of the new speakers. Both his mood and intentions were good.

He arrived in the nearby town of Tonmarket and pulled into the local DIY merchants, narrowly missing a customer and a trolley. His jovial trot to the store was almost comical. He selected three tins of whitewash and somewhat unsteadily managed to get them to the checkout. Next time he'll get a basket.

The Regulars

The young lady behind the till didn't exactly give off the air of an employee of the month but her fresh picture was there on the wall as proof. Jeff mistakenly slammed the first tin on the counter.

'Oops. Sorry love. Nearly creamed you with that stuff!'

She looked up indignantly, 'I beg your pardon?'

'The paint. I nearly dropped it on you' Jeff apologised.

She ran the order through the till routinely. 'Twenty ninety-nine, sir.'

'For that lot? Bloody hell!'

She obviously hadn't the time to argue. 'You can't put it back now, sir. I've put it through the till.'

Jeff frantically checked his pockets and managed to come up with the dough. 'Here you go. Keep the change.'

The last remark was intentionally sarcastic, but Jeff kept his confident mood all the same.

Jeff loaded the three tins of whitewash

on to the passenger seat and pulled the seat belt over it in futile attempt to secure them. He sat back in the leather upholstery, placed his mobile phone on the seat, next to the tins and thought to himself 'I'd like a bit of this,' before pulling out of the car park.

The heavy metal music was blaring out louder than before as Jeff made his way back down the country lanes. A bit of air guitar was also in order along with a singalong.

Jeff's mobile rang… 'H' appeared on the display. He picked up the phone.

'My guru… What? Already? I thought you said one o'clock. Bloody hell!' Jeff continued talking and driving and, slightly distracted, started to veer into the middle of the narrow lane. 'Yeah I'm on my way back now… No – it's got a puncture. I borrowed big Cliff's new Merc. Nice motor. He won't know. See yah.'

Just at this point, another car suddenly came into view from the opposite direction. Jeff swerved, as did the other car but, unfortunately, into a ditch as they managed to avoid each other. Jeff was still going and appeared to be okay, a little startled but no damage, so drove straight off. He managed a further quarter of a mile when he glanced down at the paint. His face dropped!

* * * *

Robin Coote was the brewery inspector. Not the sharpest tool in the box but not someone the boys needed on their wrong side. Harry was already showing him around the pub.

'This, Robin, is the main bar area as you know. As you can see, all was in order.' Harry put on the act.

The inspector looked up from his clipboard. 'Yes, very good. What's your clientele like?'

'Well, there's one of my regulars sat over there,' Harry pointed to an old man sat in the corner table with a pint on the

The Face

go. The old man subsequently pulled his false teeth out and gave them a quick rinse in the pint before replacing them. Harry looked back at the inspector hoping he was looking at the clipboard. He wasn't.

The vroom of the Mercedes pulling back into the rear car park could be heard by most of the neighbours. Jeff got out and, as he did so, a big gloop of whitewash exited the car with him and slid down his boot.

Back in the pub, Harry had pulled out a crate of ale for inspection. 'These are all in date, too.'

'Yes, that seems okay too,' another tick on the inspector's clipboard. Harry was pleased. The inspection was going better than expected.

Outside, Jeff propped a ladder against the front of the pub. He took up the two remaining tins of whitewash and placed them precariously on a ledge. Unbeknownst to him the inspector's car was directly below.

The Regulars

There then came a whistle... it was Brassie passing the pub.

'Oi Jeff!'

'What you doing, Brassie? Got the word about yet?'

'Not half. He's my ultimate hero. I've been supporting Town since I was eleven!' Brassie displayed the same old Roger Stork T-Shirt he constantly wore.

'Good man. This will put us on the map,' Jeff called down as he turned back to his paint job.

'Harry's asked me and Cliff to do the door. I reckon there's about seventy odd coming.' Brassie stated proudly.

'Wow that's cool, Brass. Well done. I must press on with this, though. See you.'

'Yeah I can't wait.'

'Neither can I, Brass.'

Jeff took up the painting again and brushed a few strokes. He then looked down to see Brassie still there, watching.

'Still here Brassie?'

'I'm too excited. I can't wait.'

The Face

'Well you can't stay there all day?'

'I'll go, shall I?'

'That would be nice.'

Brassie waved. Jeff then put his brush into the pot and started painting. He looked around to see if Brassie was still there and spotted a lovely auburn-haired lady with a low-cut top walking below him.

His eyes followed her; his open mouth able to catch any fly in the vicinity. He then tried to put his brush in the paint pot again, but inadvertently proceeded to push the pot off the ledge.

The white paint descended and splattered on the bonnet of the inspector's car.

At that moment, Harry and the inspector walked into view.

'Thank you, Mr Knocker. I'll be calling again in a few months.'

Harry and the inspector shook hands and then both turned towards the inspector's car. Both of their faces dropped like a stone.

The Regulars

They both then looked up.
Jeff had made himself scarce and was nowhere to be seen.

Confused, the inspector merely commented 'Remarkable sized pigeons you've got around here?'
Harry was speechless. 'Um... yes they are a bit, aren't they?'

* * * *

The pub hadn't yet opened for the evening. Harry was pottering about behind the bar, positioning glasses and trying to make it look just right. Julie the barmaid entered with her coat on ready to start her shift. Julie was wearing a large pair of spectacles and spoke with a broad Bristolian accent, which could be rather grating at times.

'Evening Boss.'

'Evening Julie. How are you?' Harry said with the inevitable dread of knowing what would come next.

'Well, I've had a hell of a day...

The Face

'You must tell me about it someday,' Harry responded sarcastically.

Julie continued ignorantly, 'Hubby has been out all day. He told me he was ploughing the rough fields this afternoon, and do you know what?'

Harry was managing to maintain a jot of interest, 'Go on. He's dug up the holy grail?'

'No… He only didn't go ploughing.'

'Really?' Another feign of interest from Harry.

'You'll never guess?'

Harry's had it now. 'Shot up the Champs Elysees? Skinny dipped in Trafalgar Square?'

'No. He's done them years ago. No. He went shopping. He only went and bought me a nurse's uniform. He likes it when I dress up.' Julie proudly announced.

'A Nurse's uniform? And where did he buy that?'

Julie's expression changed to puzzlement, 'Well that's the funny thing.

He had shopping bags full of other stuff, but he left it for me to find in his overnight bag. Must have been hiding it for a surprise?'

Harry tried to choose his words carefully, 'Um. Yes, I don't really think he would have left it there as a surprise for you. Maybe he didn't want you to find it at all, if you get what I mean?'

'Of course, it's a surprise. What else would it be?'

Just at that point, Jeff made an appearance, looking surprisingly spruce for once.

Harry was saved. 'Ah Jeff. Take over this conversation will you. I've got things I must do urgently, like replace the toilet paper.'

Jeff was disappointed, 'You haven't noticed, have you?'

Harry's eyes scanned him up and down. Julie interjected as normal, 'He's washed!'

'Washed, showered, shaved, Old Spiced' Jeff beamed.

The Face

'My god. What's this. The new you?'

'After our little counselling session this morning, I decided to turn over a new leaf. I've got you entertainment tonight. Painted over your sign and had a nice, clean wash.'

'Yes. The real reason for the bathing was the fact you got covered in paint earlier. That's not the only thing he managed to cover in paint! I'm surprised we are still allowed to run this pub.' barked Harry.

At that moment, Harry spotted that someone had drawn a walrus moustache on his beloved Kimberly Childe photograph that adorned the wall behind the bar.

'What's this?' Someone had defaced his beloved Kimberly's face with a felt pen!

'I always hated that picture,' posed Julie.

'Sacrilege! How dare they!' puffed Harry back.

Jeff added his worth, 'Put it this way, Harry. It is Movember! She's only doing

The Regulars

her bit for charity.'

Harry was close to tears. 'Sixteen years I've had that photograph. Sixteen years!'

'You could have got a signed one.' Jeff added.

'It was signed. It's just worn off.'

'How did it wear off?' asked Julie.

'When I cleaned it.'

Jeff looked a bit dithery, 'Why would you need to clean it? You could say it's in honour of our guest tonight. He's famous for his 'tache.'

The phone rang behind the bar. 'Could you get that please, Julie,' snapped Harry. 'I'm in mourning.'

'Good Evening... The Lazy Dog.'

Harry and Jeff burst out in giggles. Julie turned her back on them both.

'Got her again!' Harry chuckled, his mood immediately changing.

'That's the only plus having the pub named 'The Lazy Dog,' Jeff responded. 'Take the piss out of the barmaid.'

'Another enquiry about tonight, I expect?' Harry back in landlord mode.

The Face

Julie put down the phone and turned solemnly towards Harry and Jeff. 'You're not going to like this.'

Harry's eyes narrowed, 'Why?'

'That was Roger Stork's agent. He might have to cancel tonight.'

'You're joking?' rasped Jeff.

'No. He was run off the road earlier today. Seems he's got a broken arm. It was a hit and run.'

Harry was instantly annoyed, 'That's absolutely bloody marvellous. I knew it was too good to be true. What the hell are we going to do now then?'

Jeff was looking rather sheepish at this point. 'So, they haven't caught them then?'

'Didn't say.'

'Did they get a description of the other car?'

Harry interjected, 'How do you know it was another car? It could have been a tractor, hit and run, round here.'

'Oh. I don't. Yeah, you're right, Harry.'

'So, what are we going to do then?

The Regulars

We're soon going to be inundated with seventy screaming mad football fans, demanding the pleasure of an intimate evening with Roger Stork.'

A moment's silence was broken only by Julie; 'I could do a few songs?'

'You even dare go near that microphone and its cord will be used for a more sinister purpose!' blasted Harry.

'Don't blow a fuse. I'm only trying to help!'

'I could ring my mate, see if he can get someone else?' Jeff piped up.

'Jeff, we open in ten minutes!'

Julie came up with an idea, 'You could get Ernest, the Elvis impersonator, in again?'

'He won't be released for another month.' Replied Harry.

Jeff then had another lightbulb moment, 'Wait! I've got an idea. Give me a tick.'

Jeff exited, sharpish.

'Where's he going?' Julie asked.

'I have no idea. I just hope it's good.'

There was a knock at the door. Harry

The Face

called out 'It's open.' He turned back to Julie, 'I knew this was too good to be true,' and threw a tea towel on to the bar. The main door opened and in walk the normal crew of big Cliff, Brassie, Baz and Maureen. Brassie still had the word 'COCK' written in felt pen on his forehead from this morning.

Harry studied Brassie's forehead. 'Have you washed today, Brassie?'

'Yeah, why?' Brassie replied, obviously lying.

'No reason.' Harry decided to let Brassie continue as he was. Penance for previous indiscretions was his thinking.

Brassie couldn't contain his excitement a moment longer. 'Is he here yet? I'm so excited, I've wet two pairs of underpants already.'

Harry took Brassie by the shoulder, 'Well prepare to wet a third…'

Cliff picked up, 'He's not coming?'

'Exactly.' sighed Harry.

Brassie screamed and started crying uncontrollably.

'Take him out the back, Cliff. There are some tissues kicking around somewhere there too.'

Big Cliff walked up close to the bar and placed his face too close to Harry's for comfort.

'I am still getting paid for this!'

'Was that a question or a statement?' gasped Harry.

'Just make sure I do,' Cliff indicated towards Brassie, 'and this snivelling ball of puss. Where's my car keys? I left them here last night!'

'Here they are. Don't panic, you big oaf.' Julie handed the keys over to big Cliff just as Jeff entered.

'Julie. No!' screamed Jeff seeing the keys being handed over.

'What's the matter?'

Jeff backed down, 'Um. Nothing. Bazza - can I borrow you a min?'

'Have you sorted anything?' Harry asked sternly.

In the background, big Cliff lifted Brassie up with ease and threw him over

The Face

his shoulder and took him out the back. Jeff was half watching this.

'Have you managed to get a replacement?' Harry demanded.

'Er. Sort of.' Jeff then grabbed Barry by the elbow and escorted him outside.

'He worries me to death, that boy. You wouldn't think we are related.' Harry placed a forefinger to his temple to ease the pain.

'Where's he taking Bazza?' Julie asked.

'I don't know. Probably to get both their heads examined.'

Just then Jeff re-entered alone. Harry stood in front of him to block his progress into the main bar area.

'Well?'

Jeff was playing it cool. 'Don't worry. Roger Stork will be here soon.'

'Oh. So, he's coming now then?'

'Sort of. Um. Has Cliff moved his car yet?' Jeff's eyes were looking out feverishly for the big fella.

Julie replied, 'No, I've only just given him his keys.'

'Good.'

Harry then recalled; 'What do you mean sort of...?' but before he could obtain an answer, the main bar door swung open and dozens of Town football supporters tumbled in looking like they'd just moved from one drinking establishment to another.

'Is this the right pub? Roger Stork's appearing here? Tonight?' one of the more sober patrons asked.

Proudly Harry replied, 'Yes, you've come to the right place. What can I get you?'

Not quite enough information for one of the other supporters, 'Where is he then?'

Harry positioned himself behind the bar and grabbed a pint glass ready for an order. 'Not here yet, but we've only just opened.'

'I hope he buys a round,' another supporter questioned.

'I'm sure he will. What can I get you?'

'What was it? Lager's all round, lads?'

The Face

'I'll have a bitter.'

'Nine pints of lager and one bitter please, landlord.'

'Coming right up. Julie...' Harry turned to Julie, but she was already in position pulling the first pint.

Jeff now knew there was work to be done, 'I'm just going to see if he's arrived yet!'

An older gentleman looked at his watch, 'He'd better be here soon, I've got to get the train back. We're bloody miles from where I live!'

Jeff pushed passed out of the door as more supporters piled in. Fifteen... Twenty... Harry was taking orders as Julie pulled the pints.

After about ten minutes, Jeff returned, smiling broadly. 'He's here!'

'Right, can you make sure Brassie and Cliff are in position on the door before any more of this lot turn up.'

Ten more minutes elapsed and there was now absolute pandemonium in the bar as it was rammed.

The Regulars

Jeff positioned a chair in front of the main bar and then stood on it ready to announce...

'Ladies and Gentlemen. It is my very special privilege to be able to present to you…'

The noise level of the punters reduced as they waited in anticipation.

'A man that needs little introduction around these parts. He has played football in the premier league. He has won most of the honours in the game. He has appeared on the big screen with the likes of Sylvester Stallone and Michael Caine. Appearing here tonight, I give you... Mr Roger Stork.'

Thunderous applause for a few seconds until...

BAZZA appears through the door, dressed in black wig, fake moustache and wearing a retro Town Football kit from the 1970's.

The applause turned to stunned silence and then the boos started ringing around the pub.

The Face

Big Cliff and Brassie were standing outside the front door, trying to resemble a pair of bouncers. They had even donned big black coats. They could hear an almighty commotion from inside the pub: broken glass, shouting and all sorts going on.

Brassie loosened the tie he was not used to wearing, 'Cor. It's all going on in there. I told you he's my all-time hero. They must think he's amazing?'

Big Cliff was not amused, 'Yeah. Do me a favour and shut up about him. It's all I've heard all day. Roger Stork this, Roger Stork that.'

'Sorry Cliff.'

They both returned to their 'bouncer' pose. Just then a lone person walked up to the front door. His arm was in a sling. This was the REAL ROGER STORK. He went to enter the pub.

Brassie put on a deep voice, 'Sorry mate. It's one in, one out, at the moment.'

An Irish twang replied, 'but I'm booked

The Regulars

for this place.'

'Yeah, pull the other one, mate,' Cliff chipped in.

'No, I am. Really!'

Brassie went deeper, 'Who do you think you are, then? Kevin Keegan or something?'

'Mate. Hop it!' Cliff's tone was final.

The real Roger Stork turned away from the door and trotted off.

It was closing time. The place had been wrecked. The last of the evening's punters staggered past the broken chairs and tables and out of the door.

Harry looked at the empty room, with glasses and bits of sandwiches and wrappers everywhere.

'Mary's going to earn her money tomorrow!' he exclaimed.

'So did I tonight!' Julie replied, holding her wrist, 'I must have pulled five hundred pints. My arm is killing me.'

Harry didn't care, 'Even I had to pull some. Jeff, my boy you did well. We made a tidy sum tonight.'

'We did?'

'Yes. We sure did. Although I don't know if we'll ever see Bazza in here anymore. Whatever possessed you to talk him into posing as Roger Stork? I thought they were going to kill him.'

'They nearly did. Luckily, they saw the funny side in the end.'

Big Cliff entered the main bar. He had white paint dripping from his hand and an expression like thunder. Harry spotted him first, 'What's up, Cliff?'

'Who's driven my bloody car today?'

Harry and Julie both turned and looked at Jeff. Jeff turned and looked at Big Cliff, then made a mad dash out the front door.

At the rear entrance to the pub, among the crates of beer, there were a couple of wheelie bins. From one of these there came the faint echo of a muffled voice. It was Jeff, 'Cliff? Can I come out now?'

The lid to one of the wheelie bins

opened and Jeff's head appeared, covered in white paint.

'Cliff? Cliff?'

For about ten minutes Jeff's voice could be heard and then it slowly, faded away.

BED, BREAKFAST & BEER

It was very close to closing time in the main bar of the 'Lazy Dog' public house. The pub was relatively clean compared to its normal look. Julie the barmaid was holding court with the regulars: Barry, Maureen, Brassie and Cliff.

Harry and Jeff inherited Julie from the

previous incumbents. She has been at the pub twenty years, knew everyone and wouldn't shut up. It was verbal raw sewage. They called her 'The bullshit from Bristol.'

As for the regulars, there were Barry and Maureen who had both been in the village for decades. They had been engaged for nearly as long. Barry always took his seat at the corner of the bar leaving his fiancée to stand next to him. Very chivalrous was our Bazza.

Brassie was one of the many idiots the village possessed. Not very bright but spent all his wages in the pub so Harry and Jeff didn't really complain.

Lastly, there was big Cliff. He was a rugby man and could out-drink anyone. Didn't move from his seat at the table unless it was to refill his blessed pint.

Brassie tried to start a conversation with Julie based on her earlier boasting about her recent breast surgery.

'So… A thousand pounds a boob?'

'That's right. I tell you what, love. It

was well worth it.' Julie grabbed a boob in each hand.

Barry cut in, 'For you? Or the other half?'

'It's for both of us, isn't it? It's all to do with the shape. Better stimulation.'

Maureen mocked Julie, 'What shape are they meant to be? Pyramid shape?' Julie ignored her.

Brassie was still interested and dimly asked 'So how do they do it anyway? Remove a nipple, stuff the gunk in and then sew the nipple back on?'

'Oh, don't be stupid, Brassie!' Maureen cut in, 'You've seen how they blow up a football? Well… It's the same, isn't it!'

Julie stood back and removed her hands from her breasts, 'Oh my god. It's like the Suffolk village of the damned around here!'

Brassie then extended a quizzical hand intent on touching a breast, but Julie slapped his hand away before he made contact.'

'Steady on, Brassie. You'll be having a

The Regulars

stroke,' warned Barry.

'That's what I was hoping for!' chuckled Brassie.

Julie poured another pint for Barry and a large small one for Maureen. Barry paid and then asked Julie, 'When are the deadly duo back?'

'They were supposed to be back early afternoon but knowing them they've probably had an argument and one of them has copped a sulk!' replied Julie.

'They're not that bad, Julie,' Maureen said politely, 'Harry just needs to relax a little and Jeff just needs to pull his socks up.'

'You ought to tell them both that.' Barry suggested.

Harry and Jeff entered carrying their holiday bags. Jeff started moaning immediately. 'Never again. Ever.'

'What's up? Not a good destination?' enquired Julie.

Jeff dropped his bag on the floor in front of the bar and announced, 'The Norfolk broads, fine. Just don't ever expect me to go with him again!'

Harry placed his bag behind the bar out of the way.

'I don't know what you're moaning about. I wasn't the dip who left his wallet at home. I had to pay for everything!'

'Why are you so late?' asked Julie.

Jeff then threw his hands in the air, 'HE left his wallet in the B & B. We had to go back and get it. Plus, those bloody roadworks held us up.'

Harry was forthright in his response, 'The last forty-eight hours we have lived off my account. Ungrateful sod!'

Jeff countered, 'I'm not ungrateful. Look, all I wanted to do was to follow that bit of skirt into the club. No, no. We couldn't do that. Drinks are too expensive!'

'Why don't you join a dating site if your so worried about a bit of skirt?'

'I've tried. They banned me from them all!'

Harry had had enough of the excuses and turned his attention to Julie. 'How have things been, Julie? Okay?'

'So, so. Just this mob in as usual.'

Jeff rose up 'Oh so you haven't done any food?'

Julie replied honestly, 'We don't do food when you're here, Jeff!' She then recoiled, 'just a minute, the roadworks are supposed to be diverting the traffic through Sandwich Green, not away from it.'

Harry had a big grin on his face, 'yes, and everyone was so unhappy about it.'

Bemused faces all round. Barry stepped up, 'I take it you're not?'

'Nope. Think about it. More trade.'

'More food?' Jeff enquired.

'I wouldn't bet on it!' Julie's honesty came back to the fore.

'Our night away has also not been in vain,' announced Harry.

More bemused faces as no one got it.

'Well I know what we are going to do with those spare rooms we have. We do 'em up and rent 'em out. B & B style. Baz and Brassie could do them up and put a bit of brushwork on the walls. Door into the bathrooms. Sorted.'

Harry had it all planned.

'Which rooms?' Julie asked.

'The spare room upstairs next to Jeff's room and the room downstairs underneath.' Harry turned to Barry.

'Bazza me old mate...'

'No.'

'How about I wipe your bar tab clean?'

'Done.' An easy persuasion for Barry.

'Same for you Brassie.'

Julie had to cut in here, 'Are you sure that's wise?'

'It's only fifteen quid.'

'That was before you left yesterday. He came in here half an hour after you left and has been in here ever since!'

Everyone looked at Brassie who was now sat at a table grinning inanely, holding a newspaper upside down.

'How much is it now?'

Julie grabbed the book and scanned for Brassie's name.

'278 quid!'

The Regulars

'Bloody hell...' Harry thought for a minute, 'I'll let him have a couple of freebies instead.'

Jeff protested, 'Why does it have to be the room next to mine. They might hear me?'

'What would they be hearing, Jeff?' Cliff posed, already knowing the answer.

'Well, I might be entertaining.'

Julie burst out laughing. 'More like you'll have one of your mucky movies on!'

'Who told you about them? Anyway, they're not mine. They're Barry's.'

Maureen thwacked Barry round the head.

'I told you to get rid of those!'

Barry retorted, 'I did. I sold them to Jeff!'

Harry lifted Jeff's head up, 'Cheer up, Jeff. You never know, we might get Angelina Jolie in here, one night?'

Jeff's face lit up, 'Oh. I never thought of that. Birds. Cracking idea, Harry. Cracking.'

The following morning Barry and Brassie had tooled up ready for the day of decorating ahead. They were receiving instructions from Harry.

'Right, we're just going to nip to the brewery and then the wholesaler. We'll be gone most of the day so you should be done by the time we get back.'

Jeff tried to get the boys to do something for him, 'Just give the kitchen the once over if you get a chance.'

'Your priority is the two rooms,' Harry enforced, 'Only don't muck 'em up. I want them available as guest rooms tomorrow. See you later.'

'Leave it to us, Harry. No problem.' Brassie replied.

They were about to leave the room when Jeff popped up, 'Oh, can we nip to the D.I.Y. merchant. I need to pick up a drill bit.'

'What do you want a drill bit for?'

'Um … no reason.'

Harry shook his head as they left. Barry then realised he was in charge and asserted some authority, 'Well you scarper upstairs and do that room and I'll do downstairs. You sure you know what you're doing?'

Brassie was chilled, 'Yes, Baz. Just get on with it!' He then picked up a paint can and brush and waltzed upstairs.

Six hours later and Harry and Jeff entered the bar. It was eerily quiet. No one was about and the only sound was next door's cat snoozing on the window ledge again.

'Bit quiet ain't it?' Jeff broke the silence. Harry's eyebrows raised, 'That's not a good sign. Come on. let's see if the pub is still standing …'

Harry and Jeff opened the door to the new downstairs guest room to find a lovely, neat and tidy room with the bed made. The walls gleamed with fresh paint and the dirty cream door frame was now a clean white.

'It's smashing. Do you wanna look

upstairs?' asked Jeff.

'No. It'll be fine if this is anything to go by. They've done a good job. Come on, get that stew on the go. I'm going out for a quick smoke.'

Harry was not a regular smoker but sometimes needed to nip out the back of the pub to get some fresh air and sanity for a few minutes. He finished rolling up his cigarette then lit it. In the distance, Harry heard the faint ringing bell of a cyclist.

The village vicar, Father Gorn, cycled past on a nineteen-forty's style bike with a wicker basket. His black cape, flapping in the wind. He put his hand in the wicker basket, produced a miniature whisky, took a swig and then careered straight into a ditch, slightly worse for wear. Harry rushed over immediately.

'Blimey Vicar, are you okay?' Harry helped Father Gorn up who then proceeded to dust himself down.

'Oh no, Harry. It looks like it was beyond repair.'

'Oh no Father. Looks like a slight buckled wheel to me, Rev. Nothing a good, hard knee into it won't sort out. I'll get Jeff to do it later,' offered Harry.

'I don't mean the bicycle,' Father Gorn picked up a box of wine which was pouring out its contents from a piercing in the box, watering can style.'

Harry was sympathetic, 'Don't worry Father. I know where you can get another nice box of red.'

'From your pub, Harry?'

'God, no. I wouldn't drink that muck. Try the shop!'

Father Gorn was grateful for Harry's help. 'Oh, bless you Harry, dear boy. Bless you. God will be smiling on you today, my friend.'

'Do you reckon? Well, if you could have a word with him later. Tell him to throw a few quid my way, will you? Got the tax returns coming up and all that guff!'

'Oh come, Harry, my boy. Money's not everything. In fact, sometimes I believe it to be a sin. And besides, he's skint. You've seen the clothes he wears. You've got your health, Harry, that's all you can ask for.' Father Gorn then started coughing in a too much drink and too many cigars kind of way.

'Yes, well you ain't sounding too sharp, Father. Look, why don't you take it easy? You run around this village like a lawnmower run on rocket fuel. Only last Sunday they found you asleep under the church organ.'

Father Gorn picked up a dropped crucifix and placed it back in his pocket. 'It was my birthday the night before, Harry, and the Sandwich Green way was to drink your age. You know that.'

'Yes, but you're seventy-four!'

'I know. Can't wait for next year!'

'Why don't you get yourself another pair of hands? You know, to help out a bit. In fact, I know just the bloke...'

'Who?' Father Gorn asked inquisitively.

'Brass...'

'Sweet Jesus, No. I want someone...'

The Regulars

'With a brain cell? He isn't as stupid as he looks, Father. He's got a heart of gold. He did get a word in The Sport crossword the other day… It wasn't the right word, but it still fit the three spaces. Look, okay, he is bloody stupid, but he can do all the menial jobs. Polishing the church pews, lighting the candles and filling up the font.'

'Harry, you seem to forget,' Father Gorn reminded him, 'I buried his mother last year – at the second attempt!'

'Oh yes, I did hear about that. How is the Poodle now?'

Father Gorn shook his head in some thought. 'Well, I suppose it wasn't all his fault. Stringfellow's is busy on a weekend night. Anyway, I must be away. I'm not your normal nine-to-five vicar, you know. I've got an exorcism to bang out. Mrs Blackbeard reckons her living room is haunted so I'm going around to get rid of any evil spirits.'

'As well as drinking them, Father?'

Oblivious, Father Gorn continued, 'By

Bed, Breakfast & Beer

the end of the day the whole house will be haunted and at twenty-five quid a room, should be a nice little earner. Might get to PVC the vicarage windows at this rate!'

'You're full of it, aren't you, Father.' replied Harry.

'Alcohol, mainly. Take care, Harry, my friend. People to marry, babies to christen and many to bury…' Father Gorn biked off in comedy buckled wheel fashion.

Harry called after him, not expecting him to hear, 'Make sure you don't bury the bride and christen a corpse, you drunken old sod!'

Jeff was mooching about in the 'Lazy Dog' kitchen, looking busy but creating nothing. Harry walked in purposefully.

'Have you seen my jock strap anywhere, Jeff? I'm playing badminton later with Farmer Nash.'

'Cobweb Mary has washed all your badminton gear and bunged it out on the line. I told her you had a big game against that old tight arse, so I said you'd probably appreciate it, H.'

Astonished, Harry replied 'Well! I am shocked, young Jeffrey. You two have used a bit of initiative for a change. Better strap ourselves in 'cos it could be a bumpy ride!'

Harry took the lid off a saucepan on the hob and grimaced. 'What on earth is that?'

Jeff looked up from his cookery book.

'What?'

'This?'

'Well, what does it look like?' replied an irritated Jeff.

'Pond algae!'

'That's soup I did for the biddies from Masonry court!'

'That was a fortnight ago,' replied Harry in disbelief.

Jeff shrugged his shoulders while Harry shook his head and walked out to retrieve his badminton gear.

Harry stepped outside and stopped

suddenly. On the washing line were five shuttlecocks and a bent badminton racket.

'I don't... bloody Nora... she's only gone and... JEFF!'

Jeff poked his head out of the door. 'What's up? You find your jock strap, bruv?'

'Our cleaner's a jock bloody strap! She's only gone and put it all in the machine. Look at it. How am I supposed to play with that?'

Jeff took a long hard look at the knackered equipment clipped to the line.

'Err... Badly?'

It was now early evening and the regulars were in tow with Harry, Jeff and Julie behind the bar. Harry was giving Jeff another pep talk.

'Next time, do it my way, as our Grandad used to say.'

'Here, H. What was Grandad like? The only picture I have of him was the very faded one I took off Nanna's dartboard.'

Harry smiled, reminiscing about his old Grandad, 'Oh he was a real Casanova. The total opposite of you. Everyone warmed to him, especially the ladies. He had a special sort of magnetism.'

'What did he look like? My picture was so old and creased it could have been anybody.'

'He was tall, had a distinctive limp. He also had this scar from his right eye down to his mouth; and half his left ear was missing.'

'Blimey! What was it? Old war injuries?' asked Jeff.

'No. He forgot to put the guard on the food mixer!' Harry laughed.

The big oak front door then creaked and in walked three elderly gentlemen, dressed in bowling whites. They were not your usual bowlers though. The taller of the three was nursing what looked like a broken nose and was trying to stifle the flow. Blood had poured out and onto the front of his white jumper. The second, shorter man had his arm in a sling and the makings of a black eye. The third was trying to stem the flow of blood from a wound above his left eye.

"What on earth happened to you lot?" Harry asked.

The taller man replied, "Punch up on rink three! Big Brenda got arrested!"

Cliff perked up, "My wife's been arrested?

"You better run then, Cliff!" Jeff suggested. Cliff's face soured, "You're joking. That gives me more time in here!"

Julie was wiping up some glasses, "I thought you had to work later, Cliff?"

"I am. These double-deckers don't drive themselves; you know!"

Harry turned back to the bowlers, concerned. "We'd better get you lot off to the quacks! Don't want you dripping blood on my carpet. I'm getting it cleaned, soon!" and he rustled them out of the back door.

At this point a young, slender blonde of about twenty walked in. Jeff didn't notice

The Regulars

at first, too busy on his phone. Harry was first to the chase.

'Good evening love, what can I get you?'

The blonde scanned the top shelf and settled on something soft. Probably for a change.

'Hello. mmm I'd like a slimline tonic. No ice.'

Jeff looked up and did a double take. A lovely blonde. In this pub!

'Umm. I'm just going to take this up to my room…'

He then produced from nowhere the longest drill bit you have ever seen and legged it upstairs. Harry fetched the drink.

'Here you go. Pound sixty, please. Would you like a slice of lemon in there too?'

The blonde handed over the cash. Her next question took Harry by surprise.

'I also wonder if you have a room for the night?'

'Oh, we have two rooms, but they are

not quite ready yet.'

'But the sign outside?'

'Sign? what sign?'

Julie informed Harry, 'Jeff put it up earlier.'

'He's in a hurry, isn't he? Um … okay; yes, we do have a room. Julie, could you please pass me the key to room one. The downstairs one.'

As Julie placed the room key into Harry's hand, they were suddenly stunned by the sound of drilling coming from upstairs.

'What is he doing up there?' Harry wondered.

'Putting up a shelf for his DVD collection, I would imagine.' Julie chuckled, trying to be funny.

Harry turned his attention back to the blonde as the drilling finally stopped.

'Feel free to sit with my regulars.'

The blonde looked and listened in on the conversation. Big Cliff was there with a half full pint, a full pint, a short and a glass of red wine. Brassie had a lager as did Barry. Maureen was asleep. Barry was trying to hold intelligent conversation with Brassie about Brassie's mate but was failing miserably.

'I don't call losing three fingers, only a scratch, Brassie!'

Cliff chipped in, 'What was he doing, anyway?'

Brassie explained, 'Gawd knows. But I've told him to sue the manufacturer. It distinctly said on the side of the chainsaw to 'Only use when well lubricated."

Cliff and Barry looked at each other.

'Don't you think they meant the CHAIN?'

'No. That bloody thing was covered in oil!' concluded Brassie.

The blonde turned back to Harry.

'I think I'll go to my room after all.'

Unsurprised, Harry replied, 'Oh, okay. Do you have any luggage?'

'Only this case here.'

Jeff was not about so Harry asked a favour from Brassie.

'Brassie, would you be so kind as to take the case to the lady's room? Please?' Brassie looked the blonde up and down

'Yeah, alright. Let me just get my jacket,' He then slipped on his tatty old jacket which he thought made him look cool.

Brassie and the blonde entered the newly decorated guest room and Brassie placed the case on the bed. He then went to the door and tried to lean against it looking cool, like.

'Anything else I can do for you, madam?'

'Er. No. I'm alright, thanks.'

'Well if you need anything in the night, anything. I'm always in the bar.' Brassie flicked his hair suggestively and then turned around to leave, revealing a thick white stripe of gloss paint on his back from a still wet door frame.

Upstairs in his room, Jeff was drilling a spy hole about head height into his wall with his newly purchased drill bit.

The Regulars

On the wall in the room adjacent to Jeff's, there was a framed oil painting of Margaret Thatcher on the wall. The drill bit poked out of the wall through one of her eyes. Lucky, that.

Harry was trying to entertain, telling everyone about the Norfolk Broads. Julie was boring everyone about the greater experience she had there with her husband Paul. Suddenly there was BOOM sound. Everyone stopped for a moment.

'What the hell was that?' a stunned Barry pronounced.

Julie tried to be funny again, 'Jeff still 'doing it himself' upstairs I imagine.'

BOOM. There it goes again.

Harry suspected something. 'That wasn't from upstairs!'

BOOM, once more.

'It's coming from outside!'

The main door to the bar opened and lodged in the doorway was a massive, fat, bearded lorry driver, looking like he hadn't washed this month. He had long tangled hair held out of eyes by a bandana. You could tell what he last ate as most of it appeared to be lodged in his beard.

'Hi. Wondered if I could have a room for the night?' he boomed.

Julie was disgusted, 'No, we've just let it out. Sorry.'

Harry sensed a few bob, 'Now let's not be hasty, Julie. We have one room left. Upstairs.'

The lorry driver snapped it up. 'Cool. Beats sleeping in the cab again!'

Harry then noticed the driver was still wedged in the entrance door. 'Do you need any help? Getting through the door, there, Mr…?'

'Stacks, they call me. Haystacks. After that famous wrestler, Big Daddy. Cos of my size.' The big man managed to squeeze a bit more through the door then asked, 'Do you have anywhere I can throw my food wrappers away?'

'Yes, there's a bin in the corner.'

Stacks nodded back to Harry then

The Regulars

produced a huge back bin liner full of food junk. He threw it over the corner, and it knocked the bin over.

Julie was cautious and whispered to Harry, 'Are you sure it's wise to put him upstairs? Those steps are not the strongest.'

'Oh, it's okay, Julie. I think I know what Jeff has been doing with that drill. Give 'Stacks' the keys to guest room two, please.'

Julie placed the room key on the bar which Stacks grabbed immediately, this man was vile, 'Is there a MacDonald's round here? I haven't eaten for an hour. The doctor says I've got to eat regularly to keep my blood sugar levels up. It ain't easy sitting down all day driving an artic.'
Innocently Harry remarked, 'They probably meant fruit or veg, Mr Stacks.'
Stacks grimaced, 'I hate sodding fruit!'

'No Shit!' Barry added and then whacked Barry's shin.
Stacks ranted on, 'What do they know anyway? They only give you the time of

day if you're on your bloody death bed.'

Harry continued, 'There's a Burger van about eight miles away, Mr Stacks.'

'Hmph. It just took me half an hour to get out of the cab.'

Harry sensed an opportunity, 'We do food at this pub. Here, have a look at our menu.' He passed the beer stained homemade menu to the big fella, who studied it for a moment.

'Anything you'd recommend?' commented Stacks after some consideration.

'How about a treadmill?' Barry said snidely. Maureen kicked Barry's other shin!

'What do you fancy? asked Harry.

'Burger…'

'Sorry we don't…'

'Chips… Hot dog… Pizza… Ice Cream…'

'Well I'm sure my chef could recreate his best roadside burger, Mr Stacks. You know, kick it on the floor a bit...'

Stacks spotted something on the menu,

The Regulars

'What's organic?'

'It's meat, poultry, fruit and veg that's been grown naturally without the need of a pesticide. My regular Barry swears by organic produce don't you, Barry?'

Barry looked up from the sports section of his newspaper. 'Well, Maureen does, H. The downstairs bog was very organic this morning…'

Stacks was not pleased and took a leave of absence out of the door.

'You berk, Bazza.' Harry was annoyed.

'What?'

'I could have sold starter, main and dessert three times over to that blob. We triple the price for that organic junk and make a bit of profit for once!'

'But it's not organic. It comes out of a tin from the village shop.' Barry countered.

'But the blob wouldn't know that! For all his taste buds know it could be out of the cat litter tray!'

Thoughtfully, Barry replied, 'Well at least Jeff would get one good review!'

'Oh Yeah. I never thought of that.' Harry conceded.

Stacks re-entered the bar. 'I think I'll go straight up. One of the eggs I had this morning must have been on the turn.' Stacks rubbed his extremely large belly. All the regulars groaned with the thought.

'Er... Okay. Your room is just through that door and up the stairs, on the left.'

'Yeah, Cheers.'

Stacks disappeared through the door. The regulars heard the squeak of each step as he slowly, very slowly, made it upstairs. Harry and Julie winced at each other with each step, hoping they didn't give way. Then the noise stopped.

'Thank god for that,' announced Harry.

'I thought I was in for another repair job, there,' exclaimed Barry.

Just then, Jeff entered the main bar, seemingly none the wiser of this latest visitor.

'Where have you been?' demanded Harry.

The Regulars

'Busy. Just doing some alterations to my room. With these two doing the rooms up I thought I'd do mine, too.'

Harry was not satisfied. 'You must show me one day.'

Jeff looked around the room for the blonde.

'Where's our guest?'

Brassie replied to him thinking he means the latest guest, 'Stacks'. 'Just gone up, Jeff.'

Jeff's spyhole was now in place and accordingly, he came up with an excuse to try it out, 'Oh well, think I'll have an early night.'

Julie tried to warn him, 'Yes but Je...' but Harry cut her off before she could finish.'

"It's okay, Julie. Jeff's had a tiring weekend away. Let him sleep…'

A bemused Jeff then went back to his room, although a bit surprised at Harry's leniency. He closed the door to his room and rubbed his hands together ready for a spot of voyeurism.

In the room next to him, Stacks was undressed, save for a towel round his waste. He really was disgusting. He coughed up some gunk and swallowed it. Then he stood right in front of the Margaret Thatcher painting and stretched out.

Jeff placed his eye against the spyhole ready for a viewing feast.

Stacks let the towel drop and bent over forwards on to the bed.

Jeff pulled his face away from the spy hole aghast, then had to check again.

Jeff swiftly appeared in the main bar, dishevelled. 'What the hell was that in the room next to me?'

Harry laughed, 'One of our guests. What did you think it was?'

'One of them? I thought it was the bird!'

Harry belly laughed, 'I know you did, you dirty old sod. He's paid for it, too!'

'I need help.' Jeff announced and then tried to regain some composure as he headed back upstairs. He went back to his room, paced around for a bit and then decided to go to the loo.

Jeff opened the door to find Stacks sitting on the pan reading the newspaper. Stacks looked up, unperturbed, 'Evening.'

Jeff took in a short sharp breath, enough to knock out an elephant. He tried to close the door quickly but got his foot caught, and unfortunately inhaled again. He then managed to close the door successfully.

Jeff burst through the door to the main bar. Harry, Julie and the regulars turned to see what the commotion was. Jeff bolted straight over to Harry, 'They've only put the door in to the wrong bathroom!'

'What do you mean?'

Jeff pointed to Barry and Brassie, 'These two Herbert's have only put a door in from the guest room to OUR bathroom and not the one they were supposed to!'

Barry started to panic, 'Um... Brassie

did upstairs. I did the one downstairs.'

'You were supposed to be supervising,' Harry turned to Brassie, 'Brassie, what did I tell you about the door?'

Unfortunately, Brassie was by now completely plastered and, in the process of trying to understand Harry's question and deliver an answer, his pickled brain conked out and his head dropped straight onto the bar with a thud.

'How much sauce has he had today? Clearly helping himself to the tap… again!' shouted Harry.

'Well he did say he was getting the brew in… frequently.' Barry replied, awkwardly.

* * * *

The next morning, Jeff was putting glasses back on the shelves. Julie was helping Jeff, and Cobweb Mary was gently dusting the bar with her bright yellow cloth, not making a lot of immediate progress. Harry came in, having had his usual Sunday lay in.

'Morning. How are our guests? Barbie and the blob.'

'Both checked out.' replied Julie.

'Ah good. Julie and Mary, would you both be able to go to the guestroom upstairs and clean up after that thing. I dread to think what he's been doing up there?'

'Oh God. Why do I have to do it?' Julie rasped.

'I can't leave a job like that to Mary. It needs double measures!'

Julie and Mary departed, Julie muttering under her breath and Mary silent as usual.

Harry was pretty pleased with himself and lopped a bit of fluff from Jeff's collar, 'I think the guest room idea will be a success. Once the clowns put the door in the right place.'

Barry looked over the top of his paper at Harry, then back to his text.

'Yeah I need them to do a bit of filling too. A hole has appeared in my wall.'

said Jeff.

Harry was not taken in, 'You really are a muppet, aren't you?'

Jeff realised he had been rumbled and was a bit sheepish thereafter.

At mid-morning in the bar, Harry was chatting to a lady diner and Jeff came out with a food order. As he walked up to give the food to the diner, he spotted something erroneous on the dish. How did that get in there? Jeff pulled out Harrys jockstrap from the stew!

Julie reappeared after sorting the room out, 'It's all done. Only Mary can't find the remote for the TV...'

Stacks was driving his truck when he felt a bit uncomfortable. He reached under a fold of skin under his arm and pulled out the missing TV remote.

THE SNOBS

The main bar of the 'Lazy Dog' didn't generally get very busy in the early evenings. In the other bar, nominally named the 'pool table' side, there would occasionally reside the youth of the village, that is, when they were not holed

The Snobs

up in their bedrooms and glued to their computer screens with Bluetooth headphones on. But on this particular evening, a few of them had made the daring walk to the pub for a meet up. Harry called them the Sandwich Green irregulars. Jeff just called them the Twats!

They were usually a quiet and reserved bunch who made a glass of coke last all night, much to the chagrin of the landlord.

In the main bar, Brassie had bought another lager and sat down in big Cliff's usual place. He then spotted Harry looking at him, frowning and so moved to another spot.

Harry went over to the till to check the takings for the third time in an hour and noticed Julie leaning over the bar boring the hell out of a new couple to the pub. 'Julie, if you would, please.'

Julie stopped her conversation and the relieved couple went to sit at a table with their drinks, which they had nearly

The Regulars

finished.

Julie popped around the corner to see Harry, 'What's up?'

'New to the village?' asked Harry.

'Yeah, moved into the new estate last week.'

'Well, it would be nice if they were to become a regular fixture in here so can I just ask politely if you would stop talking to them, please.'

Julie was put out for a minute or two, but it was really water off a duck's back as this was not the first time, she had been reprimanded for too much chat.

Maureen and Barry hadn't been in too long and Barry was now searching for the newspaper.

'Why don't you get yourself a nice book instead of reading all that crap in the papers every day?' Maureen berated him. Barry appeared ignorant and kept searching.

'Can't beat a bit of James,' Maureen stated, hoping Harry and Julie would hear.

The Snobs

'Henry?' posed Harry.

'E.L.' replied Maureen, 'Not into all that old stuffy pretentious rubbish,' she then bit her lip, 'I like an edge to my stories.'

'But that's all whipping and pain, surely.'

Maureen gazed at Barry. 'Oh yes…'

Jeff was busy trying to be a chef out in the kitchen. He had given himself a bit of a challenge in trying to create a Crème Brulée. He fingered the pages of the cookbook eagerly as he checked his ingredients.

The kitchen door opened and in walked Harry. 'What are you doing tonight, Jeff?'

Jeff turned a page and a pained expression came over his face. He looked up at Harry and then it changed to an 'I'm in control look.'

'Bit of Crème Brulée, Brother. Thought I'd try something exotic!'

'Oh. Okay. Don't make too much as there aren't many punters in. By the way, what was it we had last night?'

Jeff recalled, 'Beef Wellington, with all the trimmings.'

Harry winced, 'Are you sure it didn't have an actual wellington in it? In particular, one that had trodden in horse shite?'

'Yeah didn't go exactly as planned. Sorry about that. My tummy's been a bit tom tit too,' replied Jeff, rubbing his stomach.

Harry nosed about the kitchen a bit longer but couldn't detect anything untoward. Jeff pressed on trying to look like he knew what he was doing until Harry departed.

Julie was behind the bar chatting as usual with Barry and Maureen, who were now on bar stools.

'He'd just opened the bag of nuts, slipped his hand in and bit straight into it.'

Barry and Maureen were finding this conversation tiresome.

The Snobs

'A nail? He bit into a nail?' Barry replied.

'Yep. He got two thousand compensation from the supermarket chain.'

'Did he cut his lip then?' Maureen inquired.

'No. It was a false fingernail. But he ramped it up a bit... Got an old letter from the dentist... changed it a bit, put in all his pain and suffering.'

'Isn't that fraud?' said Maureen.

'Well he was in pain... He's allergic to nail polish!'

Harry had come back into the bar halfway through this conversation, 'What did you do with the money?'

Julie grabbed a breast in each palm. 'I'm wearing it!'

Barry put his head in his hands 'Dear God.' Maureen slapped him.

Harry changed the conversation, 'Moving on... Brassie! Here, ain't you got an early start tomorrow?'

Brassie lifted his head up from the bar

table, 'No. Day off tomorrow. I'm emptying my shed.'

'You took a day off for that? Couldn't you do that at the weekend?' asked Barry.

'Nah. I'll be in here.' slurred Brassie.

Maureen then gave her ten penn'rth, 'You're in here every day. Why don't you take a day off from this place?'

'I couldn't afford it.'

Everyone looked blank and then decided to give up on the conversation.

Another patron walked into the bar. He was wearing a brown suit with a darker brown pinstripe. He had a faded yellow shirt on with a brown bow tie. Up top, a brown cap adorned his bald head and, placed precariously on his pointy nose, was a pair of thick rimmed glasses. It appeared that this person had been in before, because, as soon as the regulars saw him, they shirked at the sight of him.

Julie spotted him and tapped Harry on the shoulder. Harry glanced round and his face dropped. He was now face to

The Snobs

face with the most boring man in Suffolk!

'Evening, Flash.'

The others looked round and guffawed at the ironic nickname.

Flash seemed totally ignorant of the rest of the pub mocking him and just stood in front of the bar staring at Harry, until…

'Hello.'

'Usual, Flash?'

'No, nothing too bad, please, Harry. I had rather a night of it, last night. Stella shandy please.'

Harry knew that this was Flash's usual tipple, 'What were you up to last night, then?'

'Can't you tell?'

'What's that, Flash?'

'Can you not tell from my dyed hair?' Flash whips off his cap and points to the sparse bit of fuzz on top of his head.

'Which one?' Maureen suggested. Flash appeared slightly offended by this.

'I dyed my hair last night to go to the

nightclub.'

'Rock 'n' Roll,' muttered Barry.

'Good job you did that, Flash. Get into the spirit of the thing,' Harry said, trying to keep interested in the conversation.

'Yes. Thought I had better. I thought for a moment I might be a bit too old to go clubbing.' Flash replied.

'It did cross my mind.' Maureen said under her breath.

'Touch of hair dye made all the difference.'

'Good night then?' Harry inquired.

'Yeah.'

'Glad we cleared that one up, then,' rasped Barry.

Flash continued to stare at Harry. Harry thought he might be about to start another conversation so stared back for a bit. Flash then turned and wandered over to the juke box, looked at it for a bit and then walked back to the bar. Harry had been watching him the whole time and braced himself for the next piece of perplexing conversation.

The Snobs

'So, you just come in for a bit of hair of the dog?' he asked.

'No. Meeting a lady.'

Harry was genuinely surprised at that answer so delved deeper.

'What? One you met last night?'

'Yeah.'

'Well good on you, Flash. She a corker?'

'Stunning, Harry, stunning.'

'Oh right. What time was she due in here then?'

'Eight o'clock. I thought I had better be early.'

'Early? It's only six-fifteen now.'

'Just psyching myself up.'

'Well don't get too psyched, Flash. You don't want to overdo it.'

'Hmm. Perhaps you're right. Can I change that order to a lemonade?'

'You're in luck, Flash. I've only poured the lemonade bit as it is.'

At this point, a very distinguished gentleman entered the bar. It was Lord Braithwaite. Lord and Lady Braithwaite owned Sandwich Green Manor and were very well to do. The manor house itself was situated on the outskirts of Sandwich Green in the grounds of the old Bagworth wood. They were well known in the village but were not frequent patrons of the village pub at all. In fact, they were generally not well liked on account of letting everyone know that they were rich and seemingly of a higher class. No one liked them less than Maureen who immediately smirked when she spotted the Lord.

'Evening, Bernard. What brings you in here? Thought we weren't good enough for the likes of you?' she sneered.

Lord Braithwaite took a good look around the pub trying hard not to turn his nose up at anything, 'Well, I normally wouldn't frequent this establishment or grace you with my presence but I'm afraid I'm in a bit of a pickle.'

'Oh? How so?' Harry asked.

'I need some advice, you see.'

'You've chosen the wrong place here, mate!' Barry nodded over to Julie, who was adjusting her breasts. Lord Braithwaite looked over at her. 'Quite!'

'How can we help?' asked Harry, inquisitively.

'Well... It's my granddaughter's christening tomorrow afternoon at the church, and we are all going back down to the Manor afterwards, and, well, I'm afraid to say the caterers have let me down. Some sort of Flu epidemic apparently.'

'You'd like us to step in and do the catering?'

'Well, no, actually. I was wondering if, in your line of trade, you may have come across some good caterers. Is there anyone you could recommend?'

Harry replied, sensing an opportunity, 'Well, actually. As luck would have it. My brother is fully qualified. He's had full training. Sure, his appearance lets him down sometimes, but don't let that fool you. I can assure you; he works for me with the utmost dedication and professionalism…'

The Regulars

Just then, Jeff entered. 'Bloody hell... have you seen the size of that floater in trap one?'

Harry looked at Lord Braithwaite blankly.

Ten minutes later…

Harry was remonstrating with Jeff, 'You utter prat!'

'How was I to know?' protested Jeff.

Barry witnessed the earlier exchange, 'I can't believe he agreed to let you do it!'

'You told some porkers!' Julie announced.

'You'd know all about that, love,' added Maureen.

'Yes, well. Speculate to accumulate!' Harry stated, confidently.

Jeff leant against the bar, confused, 'but why have I got to go and cook at his?'

'Because I have got the Rugby boys' do in the evening. I'll have to sort out the grub for that here. You can sort Lord Muck out - only don't cock it up!'

The Snobs

'You know me. Always have satisfied customers...' At the back of the main bar, a patron then bounced a sandwich on the bar and then dipped it in his pint. 'You'd better sort the loo out then.'

Harry nearly agreed with Jeff for once, but a thought crossed his mind just in time, 'Hmm. Mary can do that in the morning. That's what she's paid for. I'll leave her a note.'

The door to the main bar opened and in walked a female replica of Flash, compete with brown suit and cap. The only difference was a small bob of mousy brown hair underneath the beige cap. She walked straight up to Flash.

'Hello, Love. What are you drinking?' the brummie accent was somewhat out of place in the Suffolk pub. Brassie and Barry started rolling about in hysterics.

Flash stood proudly, 'Harry, Jeff, I'd like you to meet Veronica.'

Harry was a little uneasy, and unsure how to act, 'Er... Hello, er... Love.'

'Hell-o. Could I please have a Bloody

Mary. Well, this is a quaint pub. Bit out of the way, though.' Veronica had a good look around the place.

'You not from round here?' Jeff asked stupidly.

'Think we'd have noticed her, round here,' added Barry.

'No. Tipton originally. Now Ipswich. I had to move with my job.'

'Oh? What was it you do?' Jeff asked, interested.

'Construction worker.' Veronica responded.

'Come, love. Let's find a nice, quiet corner,' Flash placed an arm around his twin and they both walked over to the corner table.

Cobweb Mary was in full cleaning mode upstairs. That is, she was leaning against the bath, lightly patting the basin with cloth in one hand and cigarette in the other. Slowly, she made her way over to the end of the bath and finished it off by running the tap to rinse the dust away. Her next job was one she always left until last: the toilet. This required the donning of the marigolds and a stiff brush which she withdrew from a separate compartment in her cleaning bag. Mary lifted the lid of the toilet and saw what was inside, didn't fancy it, and then closed the lid. That's enough of that.

* * * *

Sandwich Green manor was built in the sixteenth century and after the initial erection has barely had any exterior work completed on it. The lush gardens were attended to by the head gardener, Malcolm, a loyal and prized employee of the Braithwaite's, who had spent his whole working life tending the roses and the lawns. He was paid well enough for a gardener and had a small abode within the grounds. He was not a regular visitor to the pub but was genial enough.

There were various rooms within the Manor but none so large and baronial as the grand living room. There were lots of valuable looking ornaments and plates laid out on the grand furniture.

Lord and Lady Braithwaite were right at home. The lady was running through a list on a notepad and his lordship was sat down in an armchair polishing some armour with a rag and a tin of brasso. He stroked his bushy beard and then realised he had brasso on his hand and, therefore, brasso on his beard.

'Are you sure everything was ready, Bernard?' enquired her ladyship without looking up from her notebook.

The Lord was a little tired of being asked the same question, 'Virginia, dear. Yes - it's all taken care of. Although … there were one or two hitches, granted.'

'Hitches? Why? What's happened?'

'Well - there was a problem with the catering. But it's okay now. No need to worry.'

Lady Braithwaite was worried, and looked up sharply from the notepad, 'You know what happened the last time I

The Snobs

let you sort the catering out. Petra's only just forgiven you. Our daughter's wedding - ruined!'

'It wasn't my fault, Virginia. We've been over this before. I wasn't to know the chef was a borderline alcoholic.'

'He was registered blind! Didn't you check the references?' she rasped.

At that moment, the telephone rang ...

Lord Braithwaite muttered to himself, 'Saved by the bell,' as the lady picked up the phone. She answered in a false posh accent and immediately was on the attack, 'Sandwich Green Manor. Her ladyship speaking... Well... It won't do. We ordered thirty-two carnations and we only received thirty-one... and a half... Well the head fell off... Please could you send a replacement... My granddaughter was nineteen months old. I'd like it before she reaches puberty... Thank you.'

'All sorted, Virginia?'

'Only one way to deal with these people,' replied lady Braithwaite, adjusting her broach.

The Regulars

'Quite right.'

The lady was a little absent minded. 'What was I saying?'

Just then, a rather exuberant front doorbell rang...

'Ah that's right. I want no repeat performance, Bernard.'

'I told you dear. It's all sorted.'

His lordship ventured over to the grand front door and opened it. Jeff was standing there, with a beaming and gormless smile. His chef's whites were still no whiter. Out of Jeff's sight, her ladyship called out, 'If it's those awful W.I. women again, tell them NO. I am not doing a calendar!'

She arrived at the door, then proceeded to look Jeff up and down. 'This has got disaster written all over it, Bernard!'

'Oh, no dear. He comes highly recommended. Trained by Ramsey himself,' protested his lordship. 'Loud mouthed buffoon!' called out her ladyship.

Jeff was unsure what to make of his

reception, but replied, 'Me or Ramsey? That's alright. I've got all the know-how. I brought me books with me.'

'Books?' Lady Braithwaite rolled her eyes and departed back to the living room. Lord Braithwaite responded, 'It will be alright, dear. I'm sure it will be okay.'

From the distance came her ladyships reply. 'It better be or you'll need to be wearing that armour!'

The lord turned back to Jeff and gave him a hopeful smile, 'Well, you had better come in then.'

'Just show me where the kitchen is, and I'll unload me van.' Jeff replied, trying to sound helpful.

Jeff arrived in the kitchen with a couple of carrier bags full of ingredients. Waiting for him were the lord, his daughter Petra, his son-in-law Sebastian and their nineteen-month old daughter.

'Oh. Hi all. Didn't realise I'd have an audience?' said Jeff, a bit startled.'

Lord Braithwaite was amiable enough

and did some introductions, 'Everyone, this is the Chef. Chef, this is my daughter Petra, my son-in-law Sebastian, and my grand-daughter, Porsha, whose christening it is.'

Petra and Sebastian were even more stuck up than the lord and lady, and Jeff barely got an acknowledgement.

Petra then announced, 'We're going to run a little errand for mummy. We're only in the second room along.'

'Righto, mate. I've just got to unpack this and I'm cooking on gas,' Jeff responded, trying to act casual in this room of snobbishness. They all left except for lord Braithwaite, who leant forward rather intimidatingly towards Jeff, 'Just... do a good job. I don't really fancy wearing an armoured overcoat.'

Jeff tried to make light of the 'threat,' 'You better hope it don't rain then.'

'Whatever for?'

'Cos you'll go rusty! Only joking my lord.'

The Lord's eyes narrowed as he looked

round the kitchen before leaving. Jeff started to unpack his bags and place the ingredients on the table.

There were a lot of antique items in the kitchen and these had caught Jeff's eye. While he was looking at a quality vase, a toddler's hand reached up to the table and took a small bag of sugar. Jeff turned back to where the sugar should have been. Then he started looking around for it. The little hand reached up and took the mustard. Jeff looked back around and now that was gone too. Jeff looked under the table and spotted the toddler.

'Oi! You little monkey! How did you get in here?'

Jeff moved around the table to get at the toddler who then started turning on switches to appliances, including the gas for the cooker. At that point, Petra entered the kitchen.

'There you are, darling.'

'I think she wanted to give me a hand.' Jeff laughed.

Petra grabbed the toddler up. 'Yes, quite!

I hope Daddy briefed you?'

'On what?'

'My favourite dish. I simply must have it... Lobster?'

Jeff was unaware of this but tried to conceal the fact. 'Lobster? Er yes.'

Petra left with the toddler. Jeff was now a little panicked - 'Lobster? Where's my book?' and started frantically looking for the missing book.

'In the van!' and with that, Jeff bolted out through the kitchen door.

Inside the grand baronial living room, lady Braithwaite was berating his lordship once more, 'What were you thinking? That... Pub! You must have heard about them? No one eats their food!'

The lord was on the backfoot, 'but the problem... I explained it to you. They were the only available choice.'

'I will never set foot in that place again. Just get him out as quick as you can.'

'Look, Virginia. I know they've not been the best thing in the village, but I always like to give someone a second chance.' His lordship lit his pipe as lady Braithwaite continued moaning.

'That chef looks like he has never heard of a washing machine.'

His lordship attempted to pacify her, 'If it makes you happy, I'll go and make sure he is getting on as he should be. I'm sure there will be no disasters,' then he lifted himself out of his well-worn and very comfortable armchair.

'If it all goes wrong...'

'I'll be wearing a new suit, I know,' his lordship conceded as he reached the door.

With the rear door of his van open, Jeff started sifting through his battered old cookbooks.

The door to the kitchen opened and in walked Lord Braithwaite with his lit pipe in his mouth.

Jeff was checking through a cookbook and, just as he found the right recipe...
BANG!!!
The windows of the Manor kitchen

exploded outwards. Glass shattered everywhere. Jeff was staring, open mouthed at the remnants of the kitchen windows and... dropped the book.

Harry was in the kitchen of the Lazy Dog. Not a place where he was at home, even if it was his home. For all of Jeff's inefficiencies as a chef, Harry largely left the cuisine choices all to him. However, this job was a bit of a breeze for anyone. He was making the sandwiches for the Sandwich Green Rugby boys do for later that evening. He had cut all the bread into slices and had buttered each slice. His next conundrum was the filling. All the same or mix it up a bit? He decided to mix it up and opened a cupboard door: Nothing but pots and pans that looked like they hadn't had much use. Next cupboard: one can of baked beans and a packet of curry powder. Where does he keep things? Harry started frantically opening all the other cupboards trying to find something he

The Snobs

could use as filler for the sandwiches. He could hear the phone ringing and Julie answered it with her usual, 'Hello, the Lazy Dog' with the rest of the punters laughing at her. He tried the higher cupboards but found nothing but cups and saucers. 'Where was the sodding marmite?' he said to himself as he opened doors and quickly closed them again.

Julie opened the kitchen door and came in with the phone.

'I think you need to take this. It's Jeff'
Harry grabbed the phone, 'Ah Jeff. Where do you keep the Gherkins? I can't find the marmite either...'
There was a slight pause until the phone dropped from Harry's hands and landed in a sink full of soapy water.

Father Gorn ran the church like a kid in a candy shop. He was very proud of his congregation, made up, funnily enough, mainly of females. His 'flock', as he called them, were very loyal and rarely missed a Sunday service. On that afternoon the church was host to the Christening of lord and lady Braithwaite's granddaughter.

The church was rather small, and everyone was close knit on the pews. Organ music filled the air as Father Gorn held court with the toddler in his arms.

'Christ claims you for his own. Receive the sign of his cross.' slurred the vicar, steadying himself by leaning backwards slightly on the pew. 'And the godparentsh...' The word 'godparent' was too much for the vicar as his false teeth slipped out and landed in the font. He continued with the sermon regardless.

Lady Braithwaite was sitting on the pew with a face like a smacked bottom. She glanced sideways at his lordship, who sat there with a severely singed beard, which almost looked as though it was still smouldering. There was then an almighty splash, followed by a few toddler cries.

The Snobs

Evidently the Vicar had dropped the toddler into the font.

Further back on the pews sat Harry, Jeff and Julie. Harry whispered over to Jeff, 'I thought I gave instructions that we don't serve the vicar at lunchtimes?'

Jeff shook his head, 'Not me.' They both turned to Julie, who was looking guilty. They then looked at each other and simultaneously said, 'Smashing!'

All the christening guests were now sat in the dining area of the Lazy Dog Pub. All had dead pan faces.

The lord and lady were waiting for their servings. Julie trotted out with a platter of sandwiches and placed it on the table in front of their lordships. Jeff and Harry were stood behind the bar, both with anxious looking faces. Julie returned to behind the bar. 'I think you two have done rather well under the circumstances.'

'They were for the Rugby team,' complained Harry, 'Least we could do

The Regulars

for them. Although god knows what big Cliff will do when he finds out... Hang about... You're the chef – you can deal with him!'

Jeff looked shocked, 'Me? You were the one who gave the grub to the snobs!'

'That's a perk of being the manager. Delegation! My name's above the door. It's a shame time moves on so quickly. Gone are the days when you could just beat up the staff. It's all red tape now!'

Julie picked up her glass of coke, 'I expect this lot will be gone by the time the rugby lot get here anyway? Do you know, my Paul...'

Jeff cut her off, '...is actually coming in tonight? Will we actually get to meet him?'

Harry joined in, 'Or is he some mythological figure, hidden away in that thing you call a brain?'

'Push off. He won't come in here. He's not a pub man. He loves his club too much,' responded Julie.

'Club? Which club? The Barmaid's

The Snobs

daydream club?'

'The Farmer Boys' Club!' she said confidently, showing a bit of snobbishness herself, 'They all like to get together and chew the fat over their pigs and cows. Tell each other how much money they've got.'

'I thought the farm trade was going up the swanny?'

'It is. But it won't kick in for another ten years or so. They just like to whinge.'

Lady Braithwaite appeared at the bar. 'You do realise we expect a reduction?'

Julie immediately stood up for the brothers, 'They've done you a favour, Love.'

Ever the diplomat, Harry cut in, 'Um… If you can leave half the sandwiches, I'll reduce by 50 percent.'

Lady Braithwaite turned her nose up, 'Well. We'll see. They appear to be inedible anyway.'

Jeff realised the cost of his ingredients, 'Don't be stupid, Harry. There's thirty quid's worth there.'

The Regulars

'Yes, but it might save you either a kicking from big Cliff or a night of humiliation with the Egg chasers.'

The cogs in Jeff's brain went to work, 'Hmm. I see your point. Hey. Come on, let's get the table wine out for the guests.'

Harry left the bar, placed his arm around Lady Braithwaite's shoulder and led her back to the dining area.

Outside, a decorated minibus pulled up. It was full of the rugby boys in a rather raucous state. They all piled off the bus and headed toward the Lazy Dog, except one last straggler. He was naked and as the bus drove off, a ball and chain attached to his left leg came into view.

Julie spotted them before they entered the pool table side, 'Rugby boys have arrived!' she announced.

Jeff craned his neck to see if big Cliff was leading the charge, 'Time to make myself scarce...' but Harry was having none of it.

'Oh no you don't. Get in there and face

the music.' He then grabbed Jeff round the neck and escorted him to the
pool room door. He opened the door and threw him through into the next room.

Harry came back to the main bar as if nothing had happened.

'That was a bit harsh?' Julie quipped.

'His own fault. He was the one who managed to blow up the snob's kitchen.'
Big Cliff then came in the main bar, dressed in his Rugby team's tracksuit.

'Evening Cliff. How'd you get on today?' enquired Harry.

'Tonked 'em Harry. Forty-two – eight! We went steady on them. Only the two was hospital this week.' The big fella replied.

'Yes. Well done. What you drinking? Usual?'

'Twenty-three pints of lager!'

'I thought there was going to be twenty of you?'

'There is. Four pints are for me. Are the sarnies ready? I'm starving.' said Cliff,

The Regulars

rubbing his substantial girth.

Harry replied nervously, 'Erm. Yeah. Jeff want's a word with you about that.'

'Oh yeah? Where is he?'

'He's probably cowering underneath the pool table.'

Big Cliff rolled his sleeves up and necked a full pint that wasn't his but happened to be sitting on the bar. 'Righto, better go find him then.'

Harry glanced through into the dining area and spotted one of the drunken rugby players trying it on with lady Braithwaite. 'Oh my god!' He went around the bar and poured an emergency pint of lager.

The door to the bar opened and in walked Billy of the Ocean, the biggest of the village idiots. Before Billy had a chance to speak...

'Out!!' rasped Harry.

Billy turned straight round and exited.

Harry took the full pint over to the rugby player and Lady Muck and ran it under the rugby player's nose. 'Come

The Snobs

on… There's a load more of this next door…'

Harry took the pint away and began beckoning the rugby player to follow, 'Thatta boy. Come on… NO. Leave the good lady behind.'

Back at the bar Julie was pouring the rest of Cliff's lagers out. Barry and Maureen walked in and made their way towards their usual places near the end of the bar.

'Hey Jules. Busy tonight.' said Barry, looking round at all the new faces.

'You wouldn't believe it. Someone naffed up the Snobs christening, so we had to hold it in here.'

Subtle as ever, Maureen added her worth, 'Good time to bomb this place, then.'

'Maureen!' protested Barry, for once showing an ounce of decorum.

'I agree. Get 'em while they're altogether.' added Julie.

Harry returned from the other bar, slightly dishevelled.

The Regulars

'Bloody hell. It's all going on in there. 'Banjacksed' is the word. No sign of Jeff. They have probably hung, drawn and quartered him! Oh evening, Barry... evening, Maureen.'

The Pub was full but there was still room for one more as Flash arrived. Genial as ever, Harry greeted him, 'Evening, Flash. How did it go last night?'

Flash had to think about his answer. 'Not too good to be honest with you…'

'Really? She come up a bit short for you, Flash?' asked Barry, inquisitively.

'No. On the contrary.'

'Never mind, Hey?'

'She's got three GSCE's. Too many for me! A man should never go out with a woman that's potentially smarter than him.'

'So, you've binned her?' asked Harry.

'So, to speak. She kept putting me off, too. It's funny, but every time she spoke, it reminded me of my late Uncle Derek.'

'And he was also a pain in the arse!'

The Snobs

added Barry.

Harry steadied himself a little and then looked Flash straight in the eye, 'Flash, I think it's time you learnt the painful truth.'

An hour and a few gallons of alcohol later, Barry, Maureen, Big Cliff and Brassie were all sat at the bar in a full chorus of a badly sung song. But at least they were enjoying themselves. The door to the pool room opened and out popped a rugby player, with his hand to his mouth, looking for somewhere to vomit.

The noise was loud. Harry and Julie were prancing around behind the bar trying to serve as many people as possible.

A further hour on and things had calmed down a bit as most of the crowd had now gone. The place was a mess, however.

Of the regulars, only Barry, Maureen and Brassie remained. Harry was collecting glasses, in a vain attempt to tidy up. Finally, Jeff walked in after doing a disappearing act for most of the night. Harry spotted him immediately, 'Where the sodding hell have you been?'

Jeff had obviously had a few sherbet's and simply replied 'Blah, blah, blah.'

'They must have done something to you. You wouldn't have got away with it knowing the rugby boys?'

Nonchalantly, Jeff replied, 'No way. They didn't touch me.' Jeff turned around to leave again and revealed to all that the arse of his trousers had been cut away, thus exposing his perky white bum. Harry laughed, 'That's about right!'

Harry had started collecting glasses, when lady Braithwaite entered, completely drunk, with a rugby rosette pinned to her front.

'I have just come to inform you... that this is the worst establishment I have ever been in. The food, if you can call it that, is inedible! The wine is the cheapest plonk you can buy and tasted of vinegar. The bar staff are rude, there was a naked man next door, and, worst of all, someone had dropped a CIGAR down the toilet!!'

Blank faces all round, then everyone realised she meant...

'Oh, that's ok. I fished that out a minute ago.' Brassie announced.

Harry responded, 'Brassie… that was no cigar!'

THE DARK LORD RISES

Sunlight beamed into the lazy dog kitchen, as the barmaid, Julie, was scrubbing the filthy kitchen floor. Sweat uncharacteristically was running off her forehead as she breathed out a heavy sigh.

The Dark Lord Rises

'Can you clean out the fridge after that, Julie,' a voice called out. Julie threw down her cloth into the bucket of soapy water splashing the cat.

'What? after I ring your bloody neck!' she muttered.

The grandfather clock chimed Nine AM. The clock came with the pub, the brothers never bothered to check on its value, which was no doubt getting lower and lower with the more beer being spilt on it over the weeks.

Harry was sitting on a table, ashtray piling up and pulling hard on a cigarette. Nervous energy oozing off him like a burning flame. The morning never sits easy with Harry as he's always thinking about what the day may lay ahead, or more accurately, what disaster!

The creaking of the stairs indicated to Harry that his brother, Jeff was awake, who appeared not long after, wearing what could be what his slept in, or what could in fact be his day clothes. It's hard to tell.

The Regulars

'Morning H,' Jeff croaked.

'Morning' Harry replied, stabbing his cigarette out into the ash tray.

'What on earth are you up to?' asked a curious Jeff.

'This, young Jeffrey, is a fan I'm putting up in the men's toilets. I think it would be a good idea, don't you? What with all the fumes our regulars give off.'

Jeff pulled up a pew next to his brother and took a swig of Harry's coffee. 'And you're putting this up, are you? You need a proper engineer for this thing, bruv.'

Harry pulled the cup away from Jeff's lips and replied abruptly, 'Yeah? and pay him with what? Chocolate buttons? Brassie's doing it.'

Horror appeared on Jeff's face. Harry makes the same mistake time after time with Brassie. It's always a disaster, just to save a bit of moncy but in thc long run it always costs Harry more.

Jeff was about to protest when he noticed a change in Harry's demeanour.

The Dark Lord Rises

The straightening of the back and the raising of the right eyebrow always meant that something uncomfortable was about to leave his elder brother's lips. 'I'm advertising for a new Chef.'

Stunned silence followed for a moment before Jeff responded, 'A new chef? But Harry, I'm the chef.'

'Yes. That's why I'm advertising for a new one.'

'But… I'm your brother.' Jeff's lower lip started to tremble.

Harry relaxed a little and quipped 'Yes, I know. I was there at your birth. You couldn't even be on time for that, either. Me and dad waited three days for your arrival up that hospital. You know how boring dad was?'

'You can't rush quality, Harry.'

'A full day and a half were just getting that nose out! Look, it's nothing personal, it's just I've got to do something to turn this place around. Okay?'

Jeff realised that his recent culinary

The Regulars

performances had been lacking somewhat and conceded. His next thought was potentially a way back into Harry's good books.

'I can fit that fan if you like?'

'I've already asked Brassie.'

Jeff shook his head, 'Are you mad? You do know his parents signed a contract that they would never divorce because neither wanted custody of him! You need a proper engineer, Harry.'

'Look, our profit margin is non-existent. Have you seen the accounts lately?'

'No. You won't let me.'

'And for good reason!' bellowed Harry and then stopped with a start. 'Can you hear that?'

'What?' replied Jeff, bemused. 'I can't hear anything?'

'That's the trouble. Neither can I… JULIE!'

Julie appeared on all fours from behind the kitchen table.

Harry looked down on her, 'Come on.

We are paying you by the hour.'

Julie picked up the cloth again and started muttering under her breath.

* * * *

It was early afternoon in the pub and the only customers in the main bar were the old man from number six and what was believed to be his daughter. Harry scratched his chin while catching up on the sport from the local newspaper. Jeff was wiping up some glasses with a clean tea towel for a change, part of his new determination to prove himself to his boss and elder brother.

The front door opened, and Barry entered wearing a tatty old woolly jumper. He quickly hopped up on his usual bar stool. Harry hadn't looked up from his newspaper at this point.

'Glad I caught both you boys together. I might have some good news for you two.' Barry stated proudly.

Harry finally looked up, 'Oh? How so?'

'You know that plumber that lives in

The Regulars

Market street with the hairy wart?'

'He divorced her now, Baz,' replied Harry.

'Plumber?' thought Jeff, 'Leaky Luke?'

'Yeah, that's him. Leaky Luke. Well, Leaky was working on the small hall, you know, where they school the little sprogs and that. Well, yesterday morning we had a sharp frost, didn't we? Maureen reckoned it hit minus five. Stupid woman went to bed in a hat. Didn't half make an improvement. Anyway, some of the pipes had frozen in the hall so they got the plumber out first thing. Leaky Luke. And he got his blow torch out to defrost 'em. The headmaster went potty and then chucked him off the job.'

Interested, Harry responded 'Why's that?'

'They were plastic pipes! The hall's now under four inches of water. Anyway, it's supposed to be the bowls presentation night up there tonight so I know it's short notice but… could we hold it in here? Be a good forty people I reckon,

Harry.'

Jeff's face lit up 'I could knock up a few plates of my special, Harry.'

'Best not, Jeff. Some of them are rather old and we don't want to finish them off before Christmas.' Harry replied sarcastically. 'Yes, Baz, we can hold it here for you. I'll do a raffle. Yeah, that should bring in a few quid. Cheers, Baz.'

'No worries, Harry. It was either here or the Rat's head, but he's just had a new carpet put down and Mr Toom was a bit worried he might not make the toilet in time due to his gammy leg. Just a precaution you see. Right, I'll nip up and give them the good news. See you this evening, boys.' Barry slipped down a foot off his stool and trotted out of the Pub.

Harry checked his watch and turned to Jeff, 'You'll have to get the raffle prizes. I'm playing Badminton again later, but I'll be back around four, okay? Take the money from the tip jar and if that isn't enough just use your wages.'

The Regulars

'What shall I get for prizes?'

'How about as set of cricket stumps? Blimey, They're bowlers. So, you know, a bowling bag or something. The rest I'll leave to you. I can't think of everything but remember they're of pensionable age, so something to suit them, yeah?'

Harry looked round and picked up his mobile and dialled.

'Brassie? Alright mate? It's Harry. You what? Rougher than a Badgers… Till four in the morning? Yes, I know… I was with you!'

*   *   *   *

Detective Inspector Russell and his junior PC, Lancaster, were parked outside the village shop, apparently on a stakeout. The car they were sitting in is unmarked. DI Russell is in his usual mac and aviator shades. Lancaster in a suit and tie.

Lancaster took a sip of coffee from his plastic cup, 'I told you.'

'What?' replied DI Russell.

'The tall fella. The one with the perm.'

'I bet you it's a two-man job, Lancaster. Look, he has an accomplice, the dirty little rottweiler. After all she does for him. You can't trust no one in this world, Lancaster.'

Lancaster took another swig, 'Bloody hell, you're right an all. Two-man job. Wouldn't have thought that half an hour ago.'

DI Russell leant back, satisfied. 'Twenty-six years' experience. I know a bad 'un when I see one.'

'What shall we do now?' asked Lancaster.

'Five more minutes, no rush' assured DI Russell.

'You reckon it'll be murder?'

'Put a pint on it.'

'Deal.' sealed Lancaster. As he drained the remnants of the cold coffee. DI Russell sat there, motionless.

'Well… Is she dead?' the young PC enquired.

'Bit hard to say now, Lancaster. She's closed the curtains!'

'I bloody love Lovejoy, don't you, sir?'

'Love it. I've got the box set somewhere, boy. Now… back to the stakeout.' DI Russell adjusted his legs as to gain a better view of the nearby shop.

'Sir…'

Russell looked down so his one good eye was in view. Lancaster couldn't help but look at the missing one.

'Sir… It's a bit boring, though.'

DI Russell poked his glasses back up his nose, 'Lancaster, I'm afraid being a policeman isn't all Midsomer murders and Sky news. I must have spent seventy percent of my police career sitting in this seat on a stakeout. Do you know why that is?'

'Would that be your gout, sir?'

Without hesitation Russell continued, 'It's because I'm bloody good at it! There isn't a horse, hare or hound that knows we are here…'

There was then a tap on DI Russell's

window. An elderly lady is outside. Russell wound the window down.

'Hello Jack. How's the eyeball in this cold weather? Your mother told me it sticks, sometimes? Oh, I forgot to tell her I still have that casserole dish she lent me, and I'll pop it round later in the week. Just on my way to the doctors as my groin's started weeping again.'

DI Russell squirmed, 'Yes, Mrs Longboat, I'll let her know. You, er… run along now. Police business.'

Mrs Longboat slowly departed. DI Russell turned to Lancaster, who enquired, 'I can see we are well under the radar, here, sir. What are we looking for, anyway?'

The Detective Inspector glanced back at the young PC with a look of distain.

'Lancaster, for the last fortnight, I've had intelligence that we have an incumbent thief in the docile village of Sandwich Green. The village shop has grainy CCTV footage of the perpetrator in the act itself!'

Lancaster perked up, 'You mean we're after a real thief? Excellent, sir. How exciting!'

'Exactly, now keep your eyes on the sweet aisle,' replied Russell.

'Sorry, sir?'

'We're after the Penny chew thief of Sandwich Green.' DI Russell stated, proudly.

Lancaster's previous excited disposition now turned to one of disappointment.

'Sweets? We've sat outside this shop for two weeks and we're after a penny chew thief? It's hardly the stuff of legend, sir.'

Russell turned towards Lancaster and leaned into his face, 'Don't let the rat bags snowball, Lancaster. One day it's a Penny chew, then it's a can of tomatoes, next it's a TV, Microwave, DVD recorder…'

Lancaster was unmoved.

'But sir, I joined the force for a bit of excitement. The cut and thrust of a drunken brawl, picking up a gang of diamond smugglers, you know what I mean?'

A large frown came down on DI Russell's forehead as he spoke 'Let me tell you a little story,' Lancaster's eyes rolled, he's probably heard it before, 'When I joined the force,' Russell went on, 'I thought it would be all Cowboy and Indians, just like you. I started out in London, Scotland yard, you know. It was New Year's Eve, nineteen-eighty-five. I'll never forget it. I was in Deptford. A fifty-story tower block. This young man in his Thirties, all his life ahead of him, waiting to jump off. He was standing on the balcony edge. After four hours of talking to him I managed to figure out what was pushing him to take his life. I was a City fan at the time as well. Anyway, I managed to get him down and I put a blanket over the boy, and do you know what he did, Lancaster?'

Lancaster was listening intently, this one he had not heard. 'Cry, sir?'

'No. He headbutted me. Broke my nose in two places. I still get trouble with the left nostril. So, I thought sod that and moved out here.'

Lancaster tried to find the point of the story to no avail, 'What are you saying then, sir?'

'I'm saying that if you want all the excitement, then the chances are you are going to draw blood – your own! If you like an easy, dull existence, move to the sticks.'

Puzzled, Lancaster responded, 'But you

moved here and lost an eyeball!'

'I should never have gone in that bloody pub! Whoever has a darts tournament for the blind?'

'The Rat's Head do one too, sir.'

Just then, DI Russell started the car rather suddenly, 'Was it excitement, on your mind, Lancaster?'

'Well, yes. What's on yours?' replied the eager young PC.

'Your first arrest!' gasped DI Russell as he zoomed away from his parking space.

* * * *

Old Mrs Goodrum, DI Russell's mother, who lives next door to the pub, just happened to be walking her little terrier, Maude, back home when she had spotted a bit of commotion going on at the rear of the pub. Jeff was outside scratching his head looking at the lavatory wall with a look anguish on his face.

'Morning Mrs Goodrum,' Harry

The Regulars

bellowed as he walked past to get to Jeff.

'Nice day for it,' came her reply. Harry nodded back. Pleasantries over, Harry then quizzed Jeff and why he had a face like a baboon's arse.

'Don't go in there,' implored Jeff. 'I told you not to let him do it.'

Harry didn't reply and ignored Jeff's plea and immediately entered the pub.

Inside, Brassie had installed the extractor fan and was just putting on the last bits of plaster. Brassie was very pleased with his work, 'Viola!' he pronounced as Harry entered.

'What on earth…' Harry exclaimed as Jeff also entered.

'I told you, Harry. I did try and warn you, but you wouldn't listen.'

Harry had turned to Jeff but was not looking back at his lavatory wall.

'Brassie. Look what you've done to my wall…'

Brassie did not miss a beat, 'That's purely superficial, that is. Bit of pudding and it'll be all sorted,'

'Pudding?' replied Harry, sternly.

'It's what we call 'filler' in the trade.'

Harry cracked a smile, 'Well, in my trade, it's what we call 'bloody awful'. Amazing isn't it. Sixteenth century wall, that is. And in four hundred years it has withstood Six war's, the Black death, plaster lice and whatever Dulux has had to chuck at it, and in an hour and a half, this bog's breath makes it look like it's been ten rounds with Edward Scissorhands!'

A beat of silence and then Brassie finally responded, 'Well. What do you expect for twenty quid?'

'I thought you used to be in the trade?' Harry scolded back.

'Yeah, Scarpitt's D.I.Y. yard… for a week… then I got the sack.'

'Why was that?' asked Jeff.

'I got the forklift stuck in a pallet of superglue.'

Harry was still inspecting Brassie's handywork, 'Does it work?'

'No. They wrote the forklift off. Key was

The Regulars

stuck in the ignition.'

'I meant the FAN, you fool.' Snapped Harry.

'Yeah. It makes all the right noises and that,' replied Brassie, dimly.

'Well that sounds really promising. Look, we've got a pub full later. Brassie, can't you make it a bit more presentable and easier on the eye?'

Brassie scratched his head, 'How?'

'Just move away from it!' quipped Harry, 'slap some paint on it or something?'

The D.I.Y. debate was then interrupted by the beeping noise of a lorry reversing into the rear car park. It is always bit of a squeeze, although the car park is quite big, it usually has some vehicles that have been left there overnight by the likes of Barry, Big Cliff and few tractors belonging to the farmers. Brassie never got as far as taking lessons so for once it is never him that causes the rear car park traffic jam.

'We don't get a delivery on a Thursday,

do we?' asked Jeff.

'Not today, Jeff.' Harry was perplexed and sought to investigate.

The brewery lorry inched further into the car park and got as close to the back door as he could without knocking over any of the empty discarded kegs.

'Hey, hey. Mind the guttering!' shouted Harry, but the delivery driver was having none of it. 'Here, come on. I've had enough of this crap for one lifetime. Let's get this load off.'

Harry gestured for him to stop and pull up. The driver got out, apparently in a hurry, 'Alright, mate? Can you believe last week I was done for driving too quick and this week done for driving too slow?'

Harry humoured him, 'too slow?' as the driver pulled up the back-shutter door to the truck.

'Yeah, you know. Kerb crawling. They reckon I was looking for ladies of the night! What? At three in the afternoon? Got stopped by two dopey looking coppers in the village. One looked like Dirty Harry and the other… Well. A moron. I got the office on me case as well 'cos I backed into a skip.'

'I heard it was the bosses Toyota?' replied Harry,

'Same thing, innit? I'd be better off on the rock 'n roll. This is my last load then I'm ringing the office and jacking it in… Right, so you've ordered six kegs, crate of wine and four bottles of spirits?'

Harry didn't know anything about this load, 'Have I?'

The driver slipped out the delivery note quick, 'sign here!'

'Righto. Well, thank you.' Harry said as he scrawled on the docket.

The impatient driver snatched it out of his hand just as he finished and was straight back in the cab.

Jeff had casually appeared from out of the back door. 'When did you order that lot?'

Harry looked up from reading the delivery note, 'I didn't. Put it in the cellar, quick. Look at this…'

Harry handed Jeff the note. 'This was supposed to go the Rat's Head.'

Jeff shook his head, 'You can't take it here, they'll trace it back it to us. The driver will say, surely.'

'Oh no he won't,' Harry replied, 'He's quitting his job when he gets back. DI Russell may have helped us out for a change. Sounds like he's finished the poor sod off. And… anyway. What delivery? Get it moving, quick. Get Julie to help. Think, every drink we sell tonight will be 100% profit. About time we had a bit of fortune, hey, bruv? Take that invoice please, Jeff, and file it in the executive Lazy Dog shredder!'

Harry then proceeded to pick up a keg and took it inside. Momentarily he appeared once more, this time with Julie escorting him. Julie picked up one of the wine bottles and started to go back inside.

'Don't overdo it, Julie' commented Jeff. Julie stopped and turned back to him. 'I can't overdo anything. Not with my back. I've got to be quick 'cos of customers.'

That pricked Harry's ears up, 'Have we many in, Julie?'

'Um… none at the moment,' the bar bell goes off, 'wait a minute, I hear life. Must dash.'

Harry sighed and gazed down at Jeff trying to get his fingers under a keg to prize it upright. 'Come on, Jeff. Put your Back into it! Do it like this.'

Harry then decided to show the young whippersnapper how to do it and hoisted a keg onto one shoulder and then grabbed the top of a whiskey bottle with his teeth and walking back into the pub, leaving Jeff still trying to gain a handhold on his keg.

As Harry set foot into the pub, Julie stepped right in front of him as he reached the bar area.

'Look, Harry. It's the lovely DI Russell.' She then stood aside so DI Russell was directly in front of Harry.

Harry could see the white of his eye as he had removed his aviator shades and immediately gained a more menacing look.

'Hello Knocker. How's business?'

Harry tried to reply but at the risk of dropping the bottle of whiskey only managed a faint inaudible grunt.

'How is it, Knocker, that every time I walk in this pub, I smell something funny?'

'That'll be Barry,' Julie said, trying to break the atmosphere.

Harry put the keg down and placed the whiskey bottle onto the bar with the others. 'Er. Hello Mr Russell. Drink? On the house?'

'Not while I'm on duty, Knocker. And I AM on duty.'

'Oh, Okay. Hope there's nothing serious going down?'

'Well, there just might be. I was passing so I thought I'd check in as it's been all of four days since I last looked in.'

Harry winced, 'Yes, we were wondering

why you'd been away for so long? Um… So, all okay this end, you see.'

DI Russell remained silent and paced around the main bar area, brushing past the booze on the bar but not noticing anything out of the ordinary.

'Okay, Knocker. I'll call in again in a few days. Make sure you keep your nose clean,' DI Russell slapped an empty glove across Harry's chin and turned towards the front door.

Just then, Jeff entered the back door, 'Harry, we haven't got a shredder. What shall I do with this invoice? Eat It?' the keg he was carrying then slipped from his grasp, bounced once on the floor with the loudest of bangs and came to rest upon DI Russell's freshly polished left boot. Luckily the bounce had taken most of the force out of barrel of beer and did not cause any pain.

Russell looked up and smiled, snatching the invoice from Jeff's grasp. 'Well, Well. What do we have here?'

Jeff tried to cover up, 'That? Oh, that's

nothing. Just found it floating out in the back yard. Bloody litter.'

Russell wasn't fooled, 'Course you did, sonny. And I suppose all this booze came rolling down the yellow brick road? I see it's typed here: Delivery address Rat's Head, Sandwich Green. Now. Unless the Rat's Head has upped sticks and moved four hundred metres down the road, I'd say what you're doing is stealing!'

Julie tried to appease the officer, 'It's… It's a misprint. Happens a lot with my Paul's invoices.'

DI Russell perked up, 'That's interesting, too.'

Harry then took responsibility, 'No. No. It's not stealing. Just keeping it safe.' DI Russell gave them all a cold stare with that one eye of his. The other eye fixed shut.

'I think, Landlord, that you and I need to go somewhere quiet and have a quick chat.'

The Regulars

The Lazy Dog was known, on occasion, to put on a good do or two. Well. At least it was known for it once, before the boys took residence. However, Jeff had a feeling this night was going to be a good one. Granted, it was only a load of pensioner bowlers, but it had the possibility of a good night and a change from a night of listening to Barry and Maureen squabbling, or Brassie in a coma at the bar, or even big Cliff downing pint after pint without moving away from 'his' table. Because of his size no one would join him, so he remains silent most of the evening. Good company, that.

Jeff was particularly expectant of a good night because, for a change, Harry had entrusted him with a duty. That is, Jeff had been given the responsibility of sorting the draw prizes out for the evening and had just finished laying them all out on the display table when Harry walked in after his shower and immediately made his inspection.

The Dark Lord Rises

'Jeff. What are these?' he demanded.

'These are the prizes in tonight's raffle.' Jeff replied, earnestly.

'Yes, but exactly what are these?' Harry snapped, pointing at a set of dentures.

'Oh, they're Grandad's old teeth.'

'Yes. I can see that. Why are they not in his mouth?' came the curt reply.

Jeff was a bit shocked, but replied anyway, 'Because he's dead, Harry.'

'I know he's dead, Jeff. I was one of the pallbearers. What I'm saying, you buffoon, is why didn't they plonk 'em back in before they buried him?'

'Not much use to him now, Harry?'

'I know tha… God, I need a drink, already!' Harry slipped behind the bar and started pouring out a pint of Bishop's Finger.

Jeff ambled over to the bar. 'I loved old Grandad, Harry. I know I didn't see him as much as you did 'cos he moved away and that. But I do miss him.'

Harry's demeanor changed as he took a first draw on his full pint. 'He was one in a million, Jeff. At least he went out with a smile on his face.'

'That's true, Harry. Did they ever find out who gave him that Viagra pill?'

'You want one?' Harry gestured to Jeff, the Bishops Finger.

Jeff nodded. 'Please. I mean what kind of idiot gives a ninety-three-year-old with a dicky heart a Viagra? Bet they had to nail the coffin lid down?'

Harry's eyes regained interest on Jeff's prize table. 'Those are the prizes, I take it?'

Jeff nodded to confirm they were.

'Okay, so what you have laid out along with Grandad's old dentures is what looks like a commode; a thermometer; pajamas; a tin of peaches and… what is that on the end?'

'I found that in Cobweb Mary's cleaning cupboard. I think it's the end of one her old mops, but I thought we could double it up as a toupee?'

'Christ!' Harry moaned.

'What's up, Harry. Thought I'd done

well, there.'

'Yes, Jeffrey. You've really come up trumps.'

Jeff broke into a smile. 'Really?'

'No. You fool. You used all the prize money for this load of crap, didn't you?' The smile on Jeff's face disappeared.

'Only half of it.'

'What did you spend the rest of it on?'

'Lager.' Jeff confessed.

'You berk. Anyway, you're on your own tonight for a few hours. I've got a bit of business to sort out.'

'On my own? But Barry said there was gonna be forty odd here tonight!'

Harry slipped a smile of his own in. 'Don't worry. Julie will be here, helping behind the bar. Oh, and after you've done the raffle, please don't let Julie sing. You know what she's like after a few drinks.'

Jeff was crestfallen. 'T'riffic!'

'I'll only be a couple of hours,' Harry mused, 'And remember, no free beers, plenty of smiling and try not to look like you've fallen into a coma when they're talking to you.'

* * * *

The Rat's Head pub was situated on the road heading out of the village. Best place for it, Harry always maintained. The pub itself wasn't as old as the Lazy Dog but always had its own set of loyal regulars that kept it tiding over. They had the annual tug of war between the regulars of both pubs and it was always the Lazy Dog that came out triumphant, although that was largely due to big Cliff. Opposite the Rat's head and over the other side of the road, was a rather large Viburnum bush that many of the drunkards took to relieving themselves against upon chucking out time. On this night, on the other side of the bush, trying hard not to be seen, were Brassie and Barry.

Brassie rubbed his hands together to keep them warm, 'So, why are we here exactly?' he asked, through chattering teeth.

'For god's sake, Brassie,' Barry fumed, 'I've told you about three times now! It's just a little delivery Harry wants us to do. There's three free pints in it for us, he told me.'

'Three free pints? Do well. Happy days then, Baz.'

'Something like that.'

Barry poured out another cup full of black coffee from his flask. 'You want one this time?'

'No. Don't like coffee.'

'I put of bit of flavour in it. You know. For medicinal purposes.'

'Go on, then, Baz.'

Barry pulled out another cup and put a little bit in to taste. 'Here you go. See what you make of that.'

Brassie had it down in one go. 'Not bad, Baz.' He then handed the cup back for a refill.

Both had been there nearly an hour and it was starting to get a bit boring.

The Regulars

'You know, Baz,' Brassie started reminiscing, 'this isn't how I saw my life panning out. Thirty-Six years old and I'm standing in a bush on a November night, freezing my boots off. I'm sure I took a wrong turn somewhere.'

Barry sighed, 'Tell me about it!'

Brassie continued, 'I think it was when I had that chat with that career's advisor at high school.'

Barry joined in, 'Mine was in Woolworths. I met Maureen.'

'I had dreams,' Brassie carried on without listening to Barry. 'I wanted to make it in showbiz. I wanted my name in lights. I wanted to make it so one day I could have 'An Audience with Brassie Butler' on the telly. I told my teacher that and do you know what she told me?'

Barry is half listening, half lighting up a cigar. 'Let me guess?'

'She said there's more chance of me becoming Miss World. I mean, what kind of teacher says that to a young lad with dreams and ambitions?'

The Dark Lord Rises

'A realistic one?' replied Barry.

'I hit the bottle after that.'

'How old were you then?' Barry enquired.

'Then? Twenty-One. Those words extinguished all my hopes and ambitions. I became a recluse. Things got so bad I called the Samaritans. I got chatting to a lady called Floella. Hours and hours, I was on the phone to here. I went on and on. Pouring out my heart. I told her everything about my life and then suddenly the line went dead.'

'Oh? She turn out to be a wrong 'un, Brass?'

'No. I ran out of credit!'

Barry had a little chuckle to himself as the two men were joined in the bush by Harry, having finally left the Lazy Dog.

'Thank god you're here,' rasped Barry, 'Brassie's just turned sentimental.'

Harry settled into the bush, 'Yeah, He's been like that ever since they put down his Gerbil.'

Brassie snapped out of his little episode,

The Regulars

'How did you know we were here, Harry?'

'Well, this is Mrs Patel's Viburnum bush. I was wondering when it had started smoking Hamlet?'

'Shit. Sorry, Harry,' moaned Barry.

'What are you doing here, then?'

Harry loosened his tie, 'You think I'd leave you two in charge of four-hundred and fifty quid's worth of booze, did you? I wouldn't leave you two in charge of four-pound fifties worth 'cos it'd be gone in two seconds flat!'

Barry stood up, revealing all the booze that had been delivered incorrectly to the Lazy Dog, 'But why are we sitting in a bush with it?'

'Because I got a delivery earlier of this little lot. The delivery driver was supposed to deliver it to the Rat's Head opposite, but he mistakenly dropped the lot at mine, you know me. Never one to shirk an opportunity and I was gonna have them. Unfortunately, DI Russell got wind of my plan and told me to get them to the rightful owner by tomorrow morning or I get to taste a bit of the old lumpy stuff.'

Brassie had his thinking head on, 'Why don't you just hand them back instead of all this malarkey?'

'Because I'm supposedly friends with this landlord, aren't I? And DI Russell wants to teach me a lesson. He wants me to freeze my nuts off waiting for this pub to shut so I can drop it all back off. He's never forgiven me for that dart incident.'

'Well, he did lose an eye!' Barry countered.

'Should have had them shut, shouldn't he? Look. It'll be fine. The cellar's out the back. He's shutting up early 'cos he's having a night shift of decorators in to paint the pool room.'

'Why don't they do it in the day?' asked Brassie.

'Because, numbskull, unlike me, he has customers.' Harry replied.

'Hey. Quiet. I think someone's coming, now' whispered Barry, still puffing on his

The Regulars

cigar.

'Put that out, Baz!' Harry snapped.

Coming out of the light mist, near the pub, was a woman in a red coat. She appeared to be a little flustered and acting a little shifty.

'Who's the lady?' Brassie enquired.

'Looks like Edna, the church bell ringer. I'd recognize that hooter from a mile away,' replied Barry, 'Hey, what's that over there?'

Appearing out of the mist, the other side of the pub, was a small, black figure with a cape flapping in the wind. He was in a hurry.

'Blimey. It's Batman!' called out Barry.

'That's not Batman,' Harry corrected him, 'It's Father Gorn. He's the only person who goes around in a get up like that.'

'Well, whatever he's now doing to Edna ain't in the bible.' Brassie piped up.

'Yeah. Looks like the church bells aren't the only thing she plays on.' Barry added. At that moment, Brassie's mobile starts

The Dark Lord Rises

ringing with a loud and obnoxious ring tone.

Brassie immediately tried to quell the sound, but it was too late. The mysterious couple had heard the strange noise coming from the Viburnum bush and had scarpered quicker than when they had come into view.

'You tit, Brassie!' moaned Barry. Harry was more interested in Father Gorn and what he had unfortunately witnessed a few seconds earlier. The dirty old rat.

'I think Edna's better suited to the trumpet!' Brassie quipped.

'Come on boys,' commanded Harry, 'back to the job in hand. Looks like Andy the landlord's now hitting the sack. Let's get the job done and get this into his cellar.'

'Blue. Thirty-four.' Announced Julie on the microphone, back in the Lazy Dog. She is in her element at this sort of thing. An elderly man, with a short combover, ambles up to the prize table.

The Regulars

'Well done, my lovely,' Julie gives a running commentary, 'Going for the tin of peaches are you, my love? Don't blame you. Good for the digestive system.'

Jeff pulls out another ticket and hands it to Julie. 'Red... Ooh. Paul's favorite. All the legs, it's one-hundred and eleven!'

This time, an old lady gets up, who was sitting right near the prize table.

'Well done. Oh, you're going for the stool softener pills, are you my lovely?'

The old lady turns back to her husband on her table, 'What do you reckon, Len? Be useful for our Janey. She's always on about the ones in her kitchen giving her arse-ache.' The lady turns to Julie, 'What do you do? Rub them into the wood?'

Julie looked bemused, 'No, my lovely, they're for... Oh forget it. Right, we're just going to have a little intermission, where I will sing you all, my Paul's favorite song.'

Julie belted out the first word and is promptly cut off by Jeff pulling out the plug!

Harry, Brassie and Barry were walking back to the Lazy Dog, congratulating themselves on a job well done.

Harry, particularly, was in a buoyant mood. 'Well done, lads. I told you it would be a piece of cake. Let me treat you to successful couple of pints to celebrate.'

'Barry said three.'

'You what, Brassie?'

'Barry said we'd get three pints.'

'Oh. Go on then, Brassie. Three it is. Not only have we put all the booze back, we've got a nice bit of juicy village gossip. That should keep Mr. Russell off my back for a while.'

Harry turned the doorknob to the front door of the pub and entered. The place was empty, save for Julie with a loose microphone in her hand, Jeff spraying air freshener everywhere and one old man in the corner.

'Where is everyone?' demanded Harry.

The Regulars

'We're supposed to have a pub full! Why are all the windows open? Do you know how much it costs to heat this place?' Harry then caught a whiff, 'Cor blimey. What's that?'

Brassie and Barry both screwed their faces up when they also took in that nasty niff in the air.

Jeff uncapped his hand from his mouth, 'Well, Harry. Big Cliff came in halfway through. He's back from that three-day rugby tour of Brussels.'

'That's good news. He's good for business.'

'Not tonight, he isn't.' replied Jeff. 'You see, he used the loo and er… he left part of Brussels in it.'

Julie placed the microphone in a box, 'Some of the posh 'uns from the club started to moan about the smell, you see.'

'I'd have thought they were used to it.' Barry joked.

Harry frowned, 'Why didn't you use the fan?'

'That was just it, Harry. We did.' Jeff then pointed at Brassie, 'but this plonker plumbed it in wrong. Instead of sucking the air out, it was blowing it all in!'

'Right into the pub.' Julie moaned, 'It blew lady Braithwaite's wig off! Even the cat left via the window. I've never seen such a mass exodus. There were people crying!'

Harry looked around and spotted the old boy in the corner, 'but why is that old man still here?'

Julie replied, 'His sense of smell went in the blitz. Along with his legs.'

Harry could feel the rage welling up inside him but knew deep down it was his own fault. 'I knew I should never have trusted you, Brassie. You said you'd fitted one before.'

'That's true. I fitted one at my late mothers. It worked okay until the fire. God rest her soul.'

'I'll burn you in a minute.' Harry raged, 'have we made ANY money at all?'

'Sixteen quid on the raffle.' Julie replied.

The Regulars

'About eighty quid's worth of beer, although sixty of that was big Cliff.' added Jeff. Will I ever get any luck? Harry thought to himself.

'There is one thing, though, Harry.' Jeff announced. 'Those kegs you half-hinched this morning. I'd put one of them on before you took them outside. It was well out of date. Must have been a job lot?'

Harry started chuckling, then the chuckle turned to outright laughter. The others all staring at Harry and wondering what was so funny.

'I gave DI Russell one of those kegs! That's cheered me up, no end.'

'Here, Harry. We still okay for those pints?' Brassie tentatively enquired.

'Yes, Brassie. Jeff. Please pour Brassie a pint out of that keg of yours.'

The following morning, DI Russell and PC Lancaster were staking out the village shop again and have parked in the same space as the other day.

'How was the party, sir?' asked

Lancaster.

'Terrible. My belly hasn't been right ever since. Must have been the buffet?' DI Russell then lifts one cheek from the seat and breaks wind.

'Bloody hell, sir.' gasped Lancaster. 'Not again, sir.'

'Well open a window, Lancaster, open a window.'

A LARGE, STIFF ONE

It was a surprisingly pleasant late autumn evening in Sandwich Green. The starlings were going about their business picking up the scraps left by the careless chip shop patrons and Mrs. Goodrum's terrier, Maude, had escaped again and

A Large, Stiff One

was dragging a small piece of dis-guarded cod along the road. As the little fleabag was returning to its home, a large portion of the fish came apart and settled just outside the front door of the Lazy Dog. Mrs Goodrum's cat, a constant adornment of the pub window ledge, caught a whiff and sprang down for a nibble. Along the path, leading to the pub, came Barry and Maureen, who were holding hands like a love-struck couple in their twenties. Barry was bracing the cold by merely wearing his string vest under a parka, while Maureen was a little more togged up than usual.

'I hate that bloody cat!' cried Maureen as they came up to it.

'At least we know it's still alive. First time I've seen it move in months,' replied Barry as he tugged on the pub front door.

'Are you ready, Maureen? Our big wedding news.'

Maureen nodded, 'Of course I am. Shame it took you so long to ask.'

'I asked you in nineteen sixty-four!'

'Yeah, well. I was too young, then.'

'Was that my fault?' Barry countered, 'I hope they don't laugh?'

Maureen shrugged her shoulders, 'Too bloody bad if they do, now. Come on.'

The usual suspects were in the main bar, all except for Brassie, who was nowhere to be seen. Harry was wiping up the pint glasses and studiously checking for scratches. Julie was serving big Cliff his eighth of the evening and Jeff was sat at one of the tables, in his casual clothes.

The door creaked open and in came Barry and Maureen still holding hands.

'Hello, hello,' said Jeff looking up at the pair. 'Bazza must have won the lottery or something. Looks like he's in your good books, Maureen.'

Maureen looked at Jeff and then turned back to Barry and smiled. 'He's more than just in my good books, Jeff. We're getting married!'

The pub fell immediately silent. It had

A Large, Stiff One

always been a longstanding joke that the pair would never be married.

Harry dropped a glass, which smashed and straight away cursed, 'Sod it! That was the only one that didn't have any scratches on it!'

Julie beamed, 'Well congratulations you two. May I ask when the big day is?'

Before either Barry or Maureen had the chance to answer, big Cliff piped up, 'Better be soon, you're knocking on a bit!'

Barry pulled on Maureen's hand, 'I told you they'd take the piss.'

Harry stepped in. 'Ignore them, Guys. I bet they're only jealous.'

'Jealous?' Cliff replied, 'I had the sense to ask my wife when I was in my twenties. Nineteen glorious years since.'

'Yes, but Cliff.' Jeff interjected, 'You work a dayshift and she works nights. You play rugby all weekend, so you never see each other!'

Cliff pulled his pint up to his mouth. 'Like I said. Glorious.'

The Regulars

'Yes, well.' Maureen continued, 'It will be soon, actually. The fourteenth.'

Julie turned around and checked the calendar. 'The fourteenth? Of this month? That's Saturday week!'

'We had to do it then. Prices are lower.' Barry stated, ever the economist.

'Congratulations to you both,' said Harry as had started brushing up the broken glass, 'About time we had a nice celebration in the village. Where are you holding the evening do?'

'We've booked the village hall,' Maureen replied. 'We thought we'd do it up there as a change to coming in here.'

'Charming!' added Jeff.

'No. That's your prerogative. You only do it once… eventually!' Harry chucked the bin liner into the hall and rubbed his hands together. 'You'll need someone to run the bar, though.'

Barry's crooked mouth opened slightly so both his teeth were visible as he smiled, 'Yes, we were going to ask you. That okay?'

A Large, Stiff One

'Barry, my man. Of course, it's okay. However, there is one underlying thing you haven't mentioned yet.'

Barry and Maureen gazed at each other quizzically. All the blokes in the pub had mouth's as wide as the Cheshire cats as Harry gave the answer:

'Where's the stag do?'

'He's not having one!' snapped Maureen straight away. 'I've no idea what he'll get up to?'

Big Cliff didn't like the idea of being told a potential night on the lash was out of bounds so decided to stand up for his little old mate. 'You can't stop a man enjoying a few drinks on his last moment of freedom. We'll look after him, won't we lads?' there was a loud consensus of agreement. 'And of course, you're going to have a hen night?

Maureen shook her head, 'No. That's one thing I won't be doing. I can't stand half of the old bats around here.'

'Well, if you're sure, Pet?' Barry spoke in his 'soft' voice, that he used trying to

The Regulars

sound under the thumb.

'Yes. Oh, and remember you're only having the one tonight. I thought you were going to get into shape for our wedding night?'

Jeff cupped his hand over his face, trying to stifle laughter. Harry bit his lip, but Julie just burst out with a raucous laugh.

Barry frowned, 'I took up a sport, didn't I?'

'Sport? You mean you joined the bowls club. Hardly gets you a sweat on, does it? There's more life in one of Jeff's salads than there is at that bowls club. You only go for the beer!'

That touched a nerve with Barry, 'I go for the bowls and the bowls only.'

'Right. So, since when do they play bowls at eleven at night?'

Barry immediately changed the subject and turned to Harry. 'No Brassie tonight, I see?'

'No. He's here. Somewhere. Been in since about twelve. He's been celebrating, too. He's finally got himself

A Large, Stiff One

a proper job.' Harry gave the end of the bar a quick look and no sign of Brassie. 'Jeff, go and find him, will you?'

Jeff shook his head, rose, and disappeared out the back, muttering as he went.

Just then, the front door handle started to turn. In walked Flash. The regulars let out a collective groan. Cliff picked up the newspaper and held it to his face to conceal his features. Harry looked around for Julie, but she had obviously seen Flash coming and had scarpered out the back. Harry had to be nice, 'Evening, Flash. Looking smart.'

Flash was wearing the same dull brown suit he always wears, except, on this occasion, he had something different on. 'Hello. I have a business meeting in an hour. I've bought myself a new piece of attire for the event.'

Harry's eyes searched for the new item of clothing but failed miserably.

'The tie,' Flash stated, painfully. 'I'm meeting an executive who produces scart

The Regulars

leads en masse. It's his job to come and sell me the idea of buying them. Only these are not your ordinary scart leads. No. These are 'coloured' scart leads. There's red, yellow, green, gold, puce. He's coming all the way from Loafwood, to see me.'

'All the way? You could run it!' Harry tried to remain interested, 'Just look at those two lovebirds over there.' Maureen and Barry looked behind them but then realised that Harry meant themselves. 'Getting married at their age. Going to be a big moment in what remains of their lives. You got any marriage plans or big ambitions this year, Flash?'

Flash stared uncomfortably at Barry and Maureen for a moment and then replied, 'I'd like to get the undercoating done. Before Christmas, preferably.'

The moment of boredom was interrupted by Jeff returning with news of Brassie. 'I've found him. He's passed out in the toilet, again. He's well hammered!'

A Large, Stiff One

Harry shook his head, 'Cliff, he's been drinking with you again, hasn't he?'

Cliff peered round his newspaper. 'We had one or two celebratory drinks earlier, yes.'

Flash then screwed his face up. Obviously, Brassie was not to his taste. 'Hasn't that waster gotten a job yet?'

'Yes, he has. That's why he was in here celebrating,' rasped Big Cliff.

'Oh, that's good,' replied Flash. 'When does he start?'

Harry checked his watch. 'In about five hours.'

Maureen was horrified, 'He starts in five and a half hours and you've been serving him all day? What's he doing?'

'Oh, don't worry, Maureen,' said Jeff, trying to allay her fears, 'he's only putting mud flaps onto trucks from a production line. Nothing important.'

'I've got to try and make a profit, Maureen. I do run a business, too.' Harry protested.

'You better come and have a look at

The Regulars

him, Harry,' Jeff pleaded, 'He's got his foot stuck in the U-bend and his head's resting in that bucket you put under that leaky urinal.'

'Ah. That reminds me. I need to empty that!'

Flash, Barry, Maureen and Big Cliff all started retching in unison.

'Go and get him, Jeff.'

Maureen felt sorry for the poor lad and went with Jeff to recover the inebriated blighter. Barry took to his usual stool although he was a bit wary as it brought him closer to Flash and was worried about him trying to strike up a conversation. He needn't have worried as Father Gorn then graced the Lazy Dog with his presence. The holy man is like a breath of fresh air compared to the other, more cynical regulars to the pub.

'Evening all. Triple Whiskey if you would, please, Harry.'

Harry liked the vicar. Not just because he was a regular, but he was very uplifting and brought a certain wellness to the main bar every time he came in.

'Coming right up, Vicar.' Harry obtained the vicars usual shot glass and held it up to the dispenser. 'Have you heard about the two lovebirds?'

'Of course, I have, Harry. Who do you think is going to marry them?'

Jeff and Maureen appeared back in the main bar, both with an arm around Brassie, holding him up. They propped him on the end barstool, next to the vicar.

'Hello Miss Blooe,' said Father Gorn to Maureen, 'Hope you're not too nervous, yet?' the vicar then turned to Barry, 'And you, Mr Veiner. How are the nerves? Now, I'm glad I bumped into you both. If you're wanting flowers to go on the pews then you will need to speak to Mrs Thorpe, if that's okay?'

Harry passed Father Gorn his drink and this took the vicars eyes from the matrimonial pair and on to Brassie, who was still comatose, next to him.

'Good grief,' the vicar remarked,

looking Brassie up and down, 'I think I buried something like that, last week!'

Harry sniggered, 'Excuse him, Father. He'll be leaving soon. Through the window, probably.'

Father Gorn gained a little composure back, 'I thought I'd pop in here, I've got the workers in looking at that leak in the roof. I had Luke look at it last week and it seems to have gotten worse. You see, the rain was dripping down onto the Church bell, last night. Edna's not happy. She hates ringing a wet bell. It is her pride and joy, after all.' And with that, he downed his whiskey in one go, reached into his pocket, grabbed some coins and slapped them into Harry's outstretched hand. 'There you go. I like to support my local community.'

'And the community is very grateful,' replied Harry, as Father Gorn departed as quick as he had entered.

Harry checked the coinage in his hand, 'Look at this. He must think alcohol prices have stood still since the seventies.

A Large, Stiff One

And how long have we been in the Euro?'

Barry laughed, 'He shortchange you again? He's a lad, ain't he?'

Harry wasn't duly worried, 'Doesn't matter. Whatever he owes me I take back from the whip round at Sunday mass.'

That stirred Maureen up, 'That's sacrilege!'

Harry put the money in the till, 'Oh, so it's okay for him to steal from me, just because he's a man of the cloth. It's just business.'

There was then a large bang as Brassie slipped off the stool and landed headfirst on the floor.

'Take him home, will you, please Jeff.' Harry requested, without batting an eyelid.

'Yeah, sure. I'm going to help the scouts out tonight, anyway.'

'The Scouts?' Barry questioned Jeff.

'He fancies the Akela' replied Harry.

'Ooh yes. She can tighten my woggle any day!'

The Regulars

'There's always a motive to your actions,' Maureen concluded.

* * * *

A couple of hours had passed and amazingly, Flash was still in the bar, having been stood up from his executive meeting, evidently. He had just been talking to a tall, black fellow that no one had seen in the pub before. This man was dressed very well in tweed and his hair was greying slightly at the sides.

At the back of the main bar, an elderly gentleman, John, was entertaining all by playing his accordion and singing old Irish songs.

Harry had been going through the till, trying to work out what the days takings were going to be and had only then noticed the new man. He was talking to Flash. This was not good news as new customers needed preserving for, he may never come in again. Harry had better check and ambled over to the bar near

A Large, Stiff One

the two men.

Flash was in full flow, 'So you can have red ones, yellow ones, blue ones or gold. What's your favourite colour?'

The man adjusted his smart tie and stood up straight and replied in a thick, Nigerian accent, 'Are you serious? I been standing here for ten minutes and you already put me in a deep sleep!' He turned, agitated to Harry, 'Landlord. What it take to get a drink round here?'

'What would you like, sir?' Harry immediately replied, looking around for the absent Jeff.

'Malibu.'

The penny then dropped with Harry, 'Say, you're not Paul, are you? Julie's husband?'

'You would be correct. I suspect Julie's mentioned me?'

'Only about four dozen times a day. So, tell me. Have you really swum the English Channel? Backstroke?'

Paul laughed. 'Hell, no. I can't stand the water!'

The Regulars

Harry laughed. More of Julie's porkers. Barry then came to the bar for a refill.

'Much planned for Christmas, Harry?'

'Between you and me, Bazza,' Harry lowered his voice, 'We probably won't even be in here. The brewery are on our case, big time. I've used all my savings on the rent. I make sod all on the food. Even Cliff left his steak the other day. He asked for it to be done rare. Reckoned it was so rare it had probably appeared on an episode of Lovejoy.'

Barry scratched his bald head, 'Bit underdone?'

'It nearly jumped off the plate, Baz!'

'Get him some help. Some guidance.'

'I can afford another wage,' conceded Harry, 'I can't even afford ours.'

Barry pulled the bottom of his pockets out of his trousers. 'I'd like to help, Harry. But my funds are all wrapped up in this wedding.'

Harry was pleased with the gesture and thanked Baz for his consideration.

'Another Malibu, please, landlord,'

A Large, Stiff One

came the authoritative voice of Paul, who had been listening in, 'And, if I may, a quiet word?'

Harry raised the glass to the dispenser, his hand shaking a little. A new customer wants a quiet word. Not just any new customer, but a member of his staff's husband. This doesn't look good. Harry passed the drink over to Paul and ushered him over to a corner, near where John, the accordion player was playing and singing.

Harry intimated for Paul to sit first out of courtesy. As Harry took his seat, he realised he was sweating.

'So, you have money troubles?'

Harry was a little taken aback by Paul's frankness. 'How do you know? I thought you were talking to Flash?'

Paul laughed. 'Flash? Is that what they call him? I'd call him a boring twat!'

Harry had still not relaxed. 'Yeah. It's kind of an ironic Nickname. Not sure yours would catch on, if I'm honest.'

Paul's voice then took on a serious tone.

The Regulars

'Now. This is just between you and I.' The accordionist then screeched a high bit in a song which had visibly frustrated Paul, who turned to him. 'Here. Old man. Could you button it for a minute? Or at least do something a bit more modern?'

The old man halted for a few moments. Then announced, 'This is one by Dizzee Rascal,' and launched into the song.

Paul listened for a second or two, shrugged his shoulders and smiled. 'Not bad.' He then turned back to Harry and resumed his serious stance.

'I'm a successful man, Mr Knocker, and when you're as good looking as me you tend to get plenty of admirers of the female persuasion. You get what I'm saying? This Thursday, I've got two of my favourite ladies coming to see me. Not Julie, of course. You get me, Knocker? If you could find a way of keeping her busy for the whole day. You know. Well out of the way. I'll drop you a couple of grand.'

A Large, Stiff One

Harry couldn't believe it. Not only had the Paul that was Julie's husband turned out to be nothing of the hero she made him out to be, but here he was offering Harry money to keep her out of his way. However, there was one problem. 'We're all on Bazza' stag day on Thursday. It was arranged earlier. Golf day.'

Paul frowned, 'I was hoping you were a sensible businessman, like myself, Mr Knocker. But if you can do without my money then so be it.'

'Don't be hasty, Paul.' Harry pleaded. He needed the money desperately. 'Leave it with me. I'll sort something.'

'Good man.' Paul loosened up, 'Do a good job and it could become a regular thing. There's my card. Let me know by noon tomorrow,' as the big Nigerian rose from his seat, he grimaced, holding the left side of his chest.

'What's up?' enquired Harry.

'Bloody heartburn. Remember, noon tomorrow.'

'Aren't you going to finish your drink?

The Regulars

Paul looked over at Flash. 'Here. You have it. Pour it over that prat's head.' And he slipped stealthily across the room and out of the pub.

Harry sat at the table for a moment, gathering his thoughts. John, the accordionist merrily playing away close to him. 'Another drink, John?'

John smiled and kept playing.

'Here, Bazza. Any space left on that minibus on Thursday?'

Barry got a list out of his pocket and had a count up. 'Just the one, Harry.'

'Marvellous!' beamed Harry and kissed Barry square on the forehead.

* * * *

The day of the stag do had arrived. It was a reasonably sunny morning for the time of year. The minibus had arrived, and Harry, Jeff and Brassie were loading crates of beer into the luggage compartment. Barry came toddling down the road, struggling with his large bag of

A Large, Stiff One

clubs. 'Are we all here?' Barry enquired, excitedly.

'We're just waiting for your caddy. Everyone else is on board.' replied Harry. 'Caddy? I didn't know I was getting a caddy. Bless you, boys.'

Harry looked beyond Barry.

'Oh. Look. Here she comes now.'

The three of them turned around to see Julie walking towards them, dressed in garish golf gear and brightly patterned knee-high socks.

A shocked Barry turned immediately to Harry, 'Oh. God. You must be joking?

Harry sniggered, 'Nope. Well, I thought you're not getting any younger, Baz. You need all the help you can get, lugging those heavy old things around.'

Jeff struggled to contain himself, 'What is she wearing?'

'Well. At least it will go with Barry's vest.' Harry declared.

'So, I've got to listen to her harp on all day? This isn't a stag do, it's torture!' protested Barry.

The Regulars

The stag do was taking place at the Catingham golf club, a relatively short drive from Sandwich Green. It's quite a posh club, but they're usually okay, as long as you follow their club rules.

The minibus was about ten minutes into its journey. Everyone was seated on the minibus, each with a can of lager. All the men were sat in silence, since only one voice could be heard: Julie's.

'My Paul is good at golf. He'd trounce all you lot. He's good at most things. Natural ability.'

Harry and Jeff were sat on the front seat, well away from Julie.

'What did you bring her along for? It's a boy's day.' Moaned Jeff.

'I had to. Got a little earner riding on it.'

'Oh really? How?'

'Look. It doesn't matter. Just trust me. She'll be okay when she gets out on the fairway. We won't be able to hear her.'

Jeff wasn't convinced. 'I hope you're right. It's Bazza, I feel sorry for. She's

A Large, Stiff One

already nullified the banter. Look.'

They both turn around and see an audience of glum male faces staring back. Brassie, Big Cliff. Even Flash looked more bored than usual. Julie still going on without a care.

Brassie moved forward a couple of seats to speak to the boys. 'Have you got any Strychnine I can put in this can?'

'See. I told you,' said Jeff, pointing to the back of the bus, 'She's going to trash this do.'

Harry reached into his pocket, 'Don't worry. I'd already thought of that.' He then pulled out a plastic bag full of earplugs, 'Two each and pass them along.'

The minibus finally pulled into the Golf club car park and parked right in front of a sign stating, 'Town FC Golf Day.'

Brassie was first out of the minibus and instantly saw the sign. 'Oh my god. I didn't know the football club were here today, too. Fantastic!'

The Regulars

Barry had been next off the bus, 'Neither did I? Come on. Let's play golf. Bring my clubs, Julie.' Barry was getting into the spirit of having a caddy and was giving a more professional approach to everything now.

The Groom was the first to tee off amongst the regulars and was taking his time checking out the distance, 'Could I have my driver, please, Julie.'

Julie was nowhere to be seen but Barry was still looking into the fairway. 'Julie?'

Harry and Jeff both turned around and spotted Julie some distance off, talking to a stranger. 'Oi! Julie!' Jeff shouted, 'Come on. You're supposed to be caddying for Bazza, not boring the other players!'

Julie quickly finished her conversation, gave Jeff two fingers and trotted up to Barry with his clubs on wheels. 'What would you like, Baz?'

'The Driver, please.'

'So would I, love. But he's a bit young for me. Anyway, I've got my Paul.'

A Large, Stiff One

A frustrated voice from behind shouted 'Get on with it!'

Barry tried to speed things up, 'My driving iron. This one!' He pulled the club out himself. Then got into position, steadied himself, and swiped the ball down the fairway.

'We have lift off!' shouted Brassie.

Golf is a hard game at the best of times. Let alone, when a bunch of misfits have a go and today was proving no exception. Harry, Jeff and Brassie were on the third hole, looking for a lost ball. Jeff moaned at Brassie, 'I thought you said you could play this game?'

Brassie replied, frustrated, 'I thought so too.'

'Well. You haven't hit a ball yet that we haven't lost!' Harry complained. 'We're miles behind the others now. Come on. We're going to have to drop another ball. There's others waiting to come through.'

Jeff turned back and sure, enough, there were eleven cheesed off golfers

The Regulars

waiting to proceed. Harry dropped another ball and indicated to Brassie to hit it quickly, so they could move on. Brassie held himself upright, prepared to do well with this shot. 'Thwack!' the ball then sliced over to other fairway, but instead of hearing a bounce as is normal a large thud was heard, followed by a scream.

A face pops up over the hedge of the other fairway holding his head. It is Roger Stork, the Town football player. He spotted Brassie and raised his fist at him. Luckily, he was too far away to understand the words he was mouthing, although with his Irish accent, it is possible he wouldn't be understood anyway.

'I thought he was your hero?' Jeff remarked.

Brassie waved nervously back at Roger Stork. 'Hi.'

Over on the ninth hole, Flash was about to make a short putt. He was taking his

A Large, Stiff One

time, as was usual. Big Cliff was watching him and getting a bit hot under the collar about the amount of time Flash was taking. 'Take your time, Flash,' Cliff stated sarcastically, 'No immediate hurry.'

Flash was motionless. Concentration etched on his face. Big Cliff took another slurp from his can of lager, 'You do know they close the club in three hours, Flash?'

Flash was still undisturbed. He kept taking more practice swings than was necessary, then finally returned to his original stance.

'You better hurry up, Flash. I'm on my last can!'

Flash looked as if he was about to take his shot when he stepped forward and did another practice swing.

That was the last straw for Cliff, 'Sod this for a game of soldiers. I'm going back to the clubhouse. I'll get the beers in. How many of us are there?'

Flash now had to restart his stance, but

replied, 'Ten. Including Julie. Better get her a light or something?'

Cliff walked off in the direction of the clubhouse, which was way off in the distance. He passed a golf buggy, saw the keys inside and, of course, had to try it. Zoom! Off he went in the general direction of the clubhouse.

Inside the main area of the clubhouse, it was full of golfers, having finished their rounds for the day. Also, in one corner of the clubhouse, were all the Town footballers, including a bandaged Roger Stork, who happened to be closest to the bar. Cliff entered eagerly and waltzed straight up to the barman to be served.

'Nine pints of lager and one light, please?'

The barman looked Cliff up and down.

'You a member?'

Cliff was taken aback, 'No. But I'm part of Barry Veiner's Stag party. We booked it.'

A Large, Stiff One

The Barman replied quietly, 'Mr Veiner booked a party from Sandwich Green Bowls club. We don't allow stag parties.'

Cliff changed tack, 'Oh. That's right. It's for the bowls club. The stag do is next year!'

The barman wasn't convinced, 'Are you sure?'

Cliff leaned forward, quite intimidatingly, 'Yes, my good man. Now how about those drinks?'

'Okay sir. Coming right up.'

Barry, Julie and some of the others had just entered the clubhouse, having finally finished for the day.

'I'm just getting a round in.' Cliff shouted, when he spotted them.

They gave him the thumbs up and then stood by the door as Harry, Jeff and Brassie trudged in, looking deflated.

'My Word. What's happened to you three?' Barry chuckled.

Harry shook his head, 'We got to the eighth hole and then had to retire. Brassie had run out of balls! Just a minute. Where's he gone?'

They all looked around for Brassie and noticed he was trying to push his way through the crowd to get to the bar. He slipped past a portly gentleman, tripped over his walking stick and then bumped into Roger Stork, who spilled his drink down himself. Roger turned around, a face like thunder.

'You again! You've given me a black eye and now ye made me spill ma drink!' Brassie was apologetic, 'I'm sorry, Mr Stork. Really I am.'

'Take no notice of him.' Harry interjected, trying to defuse the situation, 'He's one of my regulars.' Roger Stork was giving Brassie an ice-cold look and then backed down, having judged the snivelling wreck in front of him.

'I've just got to syphon the python!' Cliff announced, pulling Brassie with him.

'Yeah. I need to drain the main vein, too,' added Jeff.

'Just stand these all up on the bar for a

A Large, Stiff One

bit, please.' Cliff asked the barman as he had placed the ninth pint in front of them. Harry decided to join them for a spot of bladder relief.

Roger Stork watched them all depart. Still smarting from being drenched in his own beer. He reached inside his tracksuit top and pulled out a hipflask and then proceeded to pour a little drop into each of the regular's drinks, positioned on the bar. 'That'll teach the buggers!'

The Police station in Sandwich green was really a converted cottage that had once been someone's home. It had been taken over and converted at the start of the second world war. When the war had finished it went for a few years, empty and unused until the Police force took it on. It had a small cell at the rear of the property which hadn't been used for the best part of two decades. However, on this particular evening, it was full.

DI Russell was taking no chances. 'No. You're not coming out.'

The Regulars

'What have we done? Maureen will go spare!' Barry cried.

'I've got my pub to run.' Shouted Harry, frustrated.

'I've got to tuck Paul in.' Julie added.

DI Russell had them all under lock and key. 'ENOUGH! You'll all spend the night here, you drunken rabble. You're all in for assault and breach of the peace.'

'Assault?' quizzed Jeff. 'Who did we assault?'

DI Russell peered over his sunglasses, 'I received a call from the club, who claim that one of their members was assaulted by a drunken party at the gold club this afternoon.

'That was you, Julie.' Harry stated.

'Me?' replied Julie.

'Don't you remember clobbering their striker?' Jeff added.

'He pinched my bum!'

Barry winced, 'He obviously doesn't score many goals then, if he tried it on with you?'

'Piss off, you prat.' Snapped Julie.

A Large, Stiff One

Harry tried using his business sense. 'Stop it. Stop it. We're getting nowhere, fast. Look, Jack. I mean DI Russell. How long will we have to say in here?'

DI Russell smirked, 'You'll all cool off until you're sober. That means seven o'clock tomorrow morning.'

A collective groan came from all the regulars except Brassie. 'Great party, this.'

Flash came up with an idea. 'Couldn't we pay the bail fee?'

'What? For all of us?' Harry barked back. 'Don't talk wet.'

'That beer in the clubhouse was rum stuff.' Barry added, thoughtfully, 'Brassie only had one pint and he was then dancing on the table in front of the footballers.'

Cliff chipped in, 'Come to think of it, we only got one round and I paid for that.'

Harry removed a shoe and then took a seat on the floor, 'There's nothing we can do now. Just wait it out.'

The others followed suit and laid

themselves out on the cell floor. It was a bit of a squeeze for ten but they made themselves as comfortable as they could until seven A.M. the next morning when they were eagerly awoken by the young PC Lancaster, excited to be dealing with, what he thought were real criminals.

Barry pulled his clubs awkwardly up the garden path to his house. Placed his key in the lock and tentatively pushed the front door open. Maureen was awake and sitting patiently on the sofa.

'Morning, love.' Barry said in his higher, sweet vocal range.

'Morning? Love? Where the bloody hell have you been?' she rasped back, angrily.

Brassie had spent twenty minutes at his lock before he had finally succeeded in gaining access to his humble abode, whereby he entered and proceeded to fall into a heap on the floor, leaving the front door open.

A Large, Stiff One

Harry and Jeff had been possibly the soberest of them all as they entered the pub at seven twenty.

'Flick the kettle on, Harry.'

'That's right. I forgot I'm your spiv.' Harry then fingered the witch to the kettle.

'Good man' replied Jeff.

Inside Julie's house. Her husband, Paul, was sat naked, save for a pair of handcuffs on one wrist and the place was a mess. He was completely motionless. The sound of Julies key broke the silence and she entered, immediately apologising without drawing breath.

'Paul. Paul. I'm so sorry I'm late, love. We had a few problems on the green.'

Without batting an eyelid, she started picking up discarded clothes from the floor and sofa and folding them up.

'Oh. Love. You could have cleared up a bit. I thought you might still be in bed?'

She placed the folded clothes on the arm of the sofa and finally looked up at

The Regulars

Paul, who had not moved a muscle in all this time.

'It's good to see you again, my love.'
No response from Paul. 'Paul? Why are you smiling at me like that? Paul?' It then dawned on Julie.
Paul was dead.

In the Lazy dog, Harry had gotten two cups out of the cupboard and had been waiting for the kettle to finish boiling when the phone rang.

'Can you answer that? I'm doing the brew.' Harry called out.

Jeff picked up the phone in the other room. The conversation was short.

'Who was that?' asked Harry as Jeff re-entered the room.

'That was our barmaid, Julie. She just got home and found her Husband, Paul. Well. As dead as a doornail. Brown bread.'

Harry couldn't believe it. 'No? seriously?'

'Straight up. She said she was talking to

A Large, Stiff One

him for about ten minutes before she realised,' replied Jeff

Harry shook his head, 'That's about right for her. Wait! He's dead? Well, that's my little earner out the window then.'

Jeff looked a little sheepish, 'That's not all that's gone out of the window. I'm afraid to say I forgot to lock the door when we left yesterday morning.'

Harry frowned heavily as he walked over to the pool room door and peered in. It was completely empty.

'You berk, Jeff.'

A WEDDING AND A WAKE

Todd the Postman walked up to the pub front door and popped a couple of letters through the letterbox. 'Odd' Todd, they called him on account of his disappearance at the end of his shift. No one had ever seen him out and about other that when delivering his letters. He had never ventured into the pub. Never been to the village shop. Never been to the church.

He lived alone in his house in Sandwich Green. He was just a bit of an oddity. He came out and mowed his lawn on a Sunday afternoon, around 3 P.M. Once he had collected his grass mowing's, that was it. He was back inside.

The outside of 'Odd' Todd's house was nothing out of the ordinary. It wasn't a large house by any means. The front door was a nice, forest green colour. The brickwork immaculate. However, a large satellite dish positioned on the front of the house happened to be the only thing slightly strange. Perhaps also, the curtains being constantly closed could be considered strange.

Harry Knocker had just sat down at his small kitchen table downstairs in the pub when he heard the letter box rattle. He took a sip of his freshly made black coffee and then lifted himself up to venture forth and collect the mail. He had picked up both letters, glanced at the first. An early Christmas card, by the looks of it and put it to one side. He immediately knew what the second letter was going to be by the fact the words 'Final reminder' were stamped on the outside in red.

Harry tore a piece off the envelope and opened it fully. Jeff pulled into view adorned in an ancient, turquoise dressing gown, that looked second hand, at best.

'What's that? Our lottery winnings?' Jeff remarked as he pulled out the corn flakes packet from the top cupboard.

Harry was still reading the letter, 'Unfortunately not. Quite the opposite, in fact.'

Jeff was now searching for the milk and not having a lot of luck, 'What do you mean?'

Harry looked up. A distressed look upon his face. 'You better get yourself a coffee, too.'

'Where's the milk? I'm not having it black. It's like drinking tar.'

'We haven't got any. I had to cancel it,

for the time being.'

Jeff tutted and then slung a piece of bread into the toaster. 'I guess the tar will have to do. So, tell me what's up?' Jeff took the other seat at the little round kitchen table as he waited for the toaster to ping.

Harry straightened himself up, having ready the letter a second time. 'I'm afraid I've got a confession to make.'

'No pay rise?'

Harry was not in the mood now for comedic comments. 'Hardly. Look, Jeff. We've been so strapped for cash and whatever we have tried to do with this place to make a bit of money has failed.'

'They were good ideas,' Jeff protested.

'I'm not saying they weren't. Well? Perhaps I am. Come on. Some of them were shocking. It's just this… I haven't been able to pay the rent on this pub to the brewery for the last six months.'

Jeff was shocked. Harry had not mentioned this to him at all. 'You're joking?'

'Nope. There's less chance of me joking about this than there is of Brassie washing his Tee Shirt!'

Jeff's face dropped. 'Oh. You are serious, then. What exactly does the letter say?'

Harry passed over the letter, 'Here, have a read.'

'Say's here, you're the occupant.' Jeff read out loud, 'So you're liable.'

'Exactly.'

'But I haven't anywhere else to go!' Jeff announced.

'Neither have I!' Harry countered.

Jeff sat in silence for a few moments and then jumped out of his skin when the toaster finally pinged, and two pieces of black toast went flying into the air.

Jeff collected the toast from the floor, put them on a plate and bit into one piece, all in a bit of a daze. 'Have you got any savings?'

Harry took the other piece of burnt toast from Jeff's plate, 'That paid the first six months of the year!'

Jeff stuffed the last, large piece into his

mouth and proclaimed, 'Then we're in shit!'

'We are, boy. Unless we can think of a plan?' Harry now couldn't face the toast and had put it back on Jeff's plate.

'Today is busy, though,' Jeff perked up, 'It's Julie's late other half's wake in the afternoon and then there's Baz and Maureen's wedding up the hall in the evening. That will all bring in a few quid!'

Harry wasn't encouraged, 'You do realise that I'm going to have to let Julie go?'

'Oh. You can't sack her! Where's your compassion? He only died the other day. Poor woman.' Jeff complained.

'That's just it. She'll have a few quid coming her way from the old man.' Harry was forming an idea, 'He was rich. She won't need the money anymore, will she? Probably a blessing that he went and died.'

'I suppose. But even so?' Jeff still wasn't convinced it was the best idea. Possibly because it would mean more

The Regulars

work for him.

'Look. It's only business,' Harry stated. 'Perhaps I should have got rid of here before now? I gave Cobweb Mary her notice yesterday, too.'

Jeff was not amused, 'So we've got to clean this place ourselves, too? How will we cope?'

Harry drained the rest of his coffee, 'Well. For a start. You'll have to get off your arse a bit more. Plus, you had better pay off your tab! It's an embarrassment that you have the biggest tab in the pub. I'm going to call the others in, too.'

'We'll lose all our regulars if you do that.'

Harry shook his head, 'We're not going to be here, in a month, if we don't do something!'

'Okay. But you can't tell Julie today. It's not right.'

'It's better if she knows sooner, rather than later. Come on. Look lively. She'll be here in a bit. I've got that replacement fruit machine coming too.'

A Wedding and a Wake

Jeff couldn't believe it. 'You're not making her work? Today of all days!'

'Nope. I've got a new bar man from now on.'

'Who?'

'You!'

'Bloody hell.'

* * * *

Harry had had a clean-up in the bar, his attempt at making it look semi-reasonable for the wake. The funeral director was soon to arrive with the coffin and, as per Julie's wishes, it was to be laid in state in the main bar for the day, so the well-wishers could come and pay their respects. Jeff had positioned himself behind the bar, now wearing a better than normal, pressed shirt, befitting his new bar man status. Harry was dusting the curtains and hadn't noticed his new barman in situ.

'Well? What do you think?' asked Jeff.

'About what?' replied Harry, without

looking around at him.

'My new shirt.'

Harry glanced over, then opened his eyes wider, 'It's one of mine!'

'Yeah I know. But you said I couldn't buy a new one.'

Harry was about to throw the dust cloth at Jeff when Julie entered, dressed all in black. 'Hiya. Was just checking that all is ready?'

'Yes, Julie. Just doing the last bits.' Harry replied, simulating polishing with the dust cloth in his hand. 'What time is he being dropped off?'

'The funeral directors will be dropping him off at midday.' Julie advised, 'I'm expecting the guests at twelve-thirty.'

'Guests?' quizzed Jeff.

'Yes. We're going to do the wake this afternoon, before he's buried.'

'Sorry, Jeff.' Harry apologised, 'Change of plan. He was going to lie in state, and we'd have a few people popping in over the course of the afternoon, to pay their respects. Only Julie's decided to have the wake this afternoon instead of tomorrow.'

'Father Gorn couldn't fit him in today, Too busy!' Julie added, 'but it would have been Paul's Fifty fifth birthday today, so I thought it better to celebrate his life today. Right, I must dash. I've an appointment at the solicitors at eleven forty-five so I might not be back when they drop him off.'

Harry threw the dust cloth onto the bar in front of Jeff and snapped 'Your turn.' and slipped out of the door.

Julie's eyes had followed harry out of the door and then turned back to Jeff, 'What's up with him? He's a bit grumpy?'

Jeff picked up the dust cloth and placed it under the bar counter with no intention of doing any dusting. 'To tell you the truth, Julie. We've had a bit of bad news from the brewery. He hasn't paid the rent for six months and we've got to rustle up four grand or we get kicked out.'

Julie was startled, 'Oh that is bad news.

The Regulars

What are you going to do, then?'

They were interrupted by the front door banging open and a delivery chap wheeling in a new fruit machine on a sack barrow. Harry had followed in behind.

'Where do you want this, mate?' asked the delivery man.

'Just over there, please.' advised Harry, Can I just check the replacement one out? The old when kept paying out!'

Jeff and Julie looked at each other in bemusement. 'Right,' announced Julie, 'I've gotta go. Got that appointment at the solicitors. You sure you're okay to take him in if I'm not back in time?'

'Yes, of course.' replied Harry, keeping a stern eye on the delivery man as he plugged in the new fruit machine.

Jeff had watched her depart out of the window. 'Enjoy your inheritance. You lucky old bat!'

'Have a heart, Jeff. Have a heart.' Harry replied.

'Says the man who is going to give her

A Wedding and a Wake

the boot.' Jeff moved back to his position behind the bar, 'Why don't you marry her, Harry. That'll solve the money issue.'

'I wouldn't touch it with yours, Jeff.'

'No. Neither would I.' Jeff agreed. 'Still. Money would be nice.'

'I agree, but that was one poor widower who won't be getting a sausage in her hamper!' Harry replied, sarcastically.

'So. Why didn't you tell her she was being released?'

'Couldn't just yet, could I?' Harry shirked. Jeff chuckled, 'Thought you said it was just business?'

The delivery guy cut in, 'Right. I'm all done. All wired and plugged in.'

'Thank you.' replied Harry. 'Now I'm not going to lose a fortune on it, like the last one?'

The delivery guy gave Jeff a 'what is he on about?' look. 'No, mate. Should get you five hundred, If, you've got the trade?'

A smartly dressed man had entered the

pub, Harry glanced over at him, 'Hello. I'm Ryan Abbott, from Mills and Rich funeral directors. We've brought the deceased, on behalf of Julie.'

The delivery guy then squared up to Harry, 'I'd half that amount, now, if I were you, mate!' and carried the old fruit machine out of the pub, just as the coffin was being brought in.

'Where would you like him?' asked Mr Abbott.

'Oh. Stick him in that corner if you would.' Harry gestured to Jeff, 'Go and get the sandwiches and stuff.'

The two man carried the coffin, carefully, into the main bar. Another man followed in and then set up the bench, in the corner, to set it on. The other two men then lowered the coffin slowly onto the bench.

'Will that be all, sir?'

Harry didn't know what Julie's plans were but replied, trusting everything was alright, 'Yes. Thank you.'

'Good day, sir.' All three men departed,

respectfully.

Jeff then entered the bar with two plates of sandwiches and promptly placed them on top of the coffin.

'Oi!' shouted Harry, 'What the hell do you think you're doing? Have some respect!'

Jeff grabbed both plates quickly. 'Sorry, Boss!'

* * * *

The main bar of the Lazy Dog was full of mourners, in to pay their respects. The sandwiches were now all laid out on separate tables. No one had sampled any. There was little chat but what little there was came to a halt as Julie entered. One of the guests tried to shake her hand but she refused without saying a word. There was silence for a minute or two as it appeared Julie was too overcome by grief. Bert Smith, the butcher, took up the baton.

'Er. On behalf of Julie,' Bert glanced

over at Julie, hoping to get her blessing to start. She nodded back. Bert continued, 'Can I just thank everyone for coming today. Paul would have been pleased to see so many of you here to give him a good send off. There's sandwiches and rolls here to enjoy.' Bert then remembered where he was, 'Um. There are drinks, anyway. So…' He picked up a glass. 'Here's to Paul.' The rest of the group gave out a faint murmur of appreciation.

Half an hour had passed and at least a few of the sandwiches had been started. Julie was sat in the corner. Keeping away from everyone it seemed. Harry decided to take a chance. 'Julie. Could I have a quick word, please?'

'Go on then.'

'I don't mean here, Just out the back, if that's okay?'

Julie was up for it. It wasn't like she was enjoying being in that room.

Harry had taken her into the now

relatively bare pool room.

'Take a seat. I know this isn't really the timer nor place… But… I thought… Well. I'm sure you'd rather know now than…'

'What's up?' Julie asked, getting impatient.

'Well. We've kind of got a cash flow situation, stroke, problem.' Harry eventually got it out.

'Yes. I know.'

'Oh. How?'

'Jeff told me.'

Harry stroked a small bit of stubble on his chin. 'Did he now? Okay. Well. I'm struggling to pay for things around here.'

'Yes?'

'Well. I need to make some cuts.'

'Yes. Go on.'

'Staff cuts.'

'And…'

'Let me put it like this…'

The penny dropped.

'You're getting rid of me?'

Harry was pleased that Julie had finally

The Regulars

understood what he had badly tried to get out, but also terrified at the response.

'Well. Yes.'

'Nice one.'

That reply came as a surprise to Harry as he then tried to justify his position.

'I just thought… the old man might have, er… Left you a bit. Wouldn't come as such of a blow, if you know what I mean?'

Julie had listened to the reply and sat, staring at Harry in silence. Finally, she spoke.

'Actually, I do know what you mean. Excuse me. I need to address the guests.'

She slipped off the stool and casually left the room. Seemingly in a better state than she had arrived.

Harry had joined his brother, Jeff, behind the bar. Julie was about to address the guests, who were all seated.

Jeff leaned over to Harry and whispered in his ear, 'Have you done it?'

'Yep. All done' Harry whispered back.

'How did that go?

'Surprisingly well, actually.'
Jeff pulled back from Harry's ear, a little shocked at the response but otherwise pleased no offense had been taken.
Julie clapped her hands together to get everyone's attention.

'May I thank you all for coming today. I know the old fart would have loved the fact that you could all be bothered. Today has been a funny sort of day, really. They say that in times of trouble, you find out who your friends are, and I think I have today. About two minutes ago, I found out I have just been sacked from working in this pub.' A collective groan from all the guests and Harry had to turn away from Mrs Dewis, who was giving him a death stare. 'A Pub I have been working in for the past twenty-one years.' There came an even bigger groan from the guests. 'I also found something else out earlier today. My beloved Husband… I went to the solicitors this morning. What a sweetie. Well he left me a little lump sum. When I say little, well,

The Regulars

I mean little! All the money he's got, and he leaves me a piddling five grand.' Even more groaning from the guests. 'Seems he decided to share it with some other people. Well, when I say other people, I mean his fancy women. Yvonne…'

A female mourner burst into tears, rose from her seat and then quickly jolted out of the pub.

'Grace…' Another woman stood up, looked around nervously and decided it was best to leave, also.

'Any more of you?' demanded Julie.

Another four women slowly stood up and sauntered out. As they were leaving the pub, an old bloke decided to get up and leave as well.

There was silence for a few seconds from the remainder of the congregation until Grace's husband spoke out,

'I bloody wondered where Grace got that coat from?'

'Hmmm. Same with that bracelet Yvonne got!' said another bloke.

Julie and the remaining guests all then

A Wedding and a Wake

bustled out of the pub. They had decided to leave all their empty glasses on the coffin, in disgust.

Harry and Jeff had witnessed the whole episode from the relative safety of the bar.

'Well, that could have gone better!' quipped Jeff.

'That's not the only problem. What are we going to do with him?' Harry nodded over to the corner where the coffin stood. Other than the empty glasses sitting on top, it looked nice and tidy. However, totally unbefitting for the pub! 'Julie was supposed to be getting him taken away again, but it doesn't sound like she gives much of a toss, now!'

'Brilliant!' replied Jeff in his usual sarcastic manner. 'That's just great!'

'Yeah. Things are certainly going from bad to worse, at the moment.' Harry mused, 'We've got no barmaid… no cleaner… no future…'

'No Fosters!' Jeff had tried to pull a pint, but it merely filled with froth.

The Regulars

'Look. It's Saturday and there's only me, you and a coffin in.' Harry had started to rub his temple to ease the pain.

'We've booked worse entertainment, Harry.' Jeff was doing his best to make light of the situation.

Harry sat down on a bar stool, to think things through. The financial situation raised this morning had been complicated by a mere inconvenience, hadn't it? Just the little issue of having a dead body in the pub. It needs to be hidden, somewhere, just until the burial, tomorrow. Harry glanced up and through the window, spotted the genial figure of Father Gorn, heading for the pub front door.

'Ah. The Vicar's coming in.' Harry had an idea, 'I'll see if we can bung him in the church for the night.'

'Blimey, Harry. That's was someone's body. Not a Chinese takeaway!'

The door burst open with Father Gorns usual anticipation.

'Hello Harry and Jeff. I can't stop long,'

the vicar seemed to be in a hurry, 'I'd just like to say what a wonderful thing you did, letting Julie hold the wake in here.'

'Yes, but…'

The vicar continued rapidly, 'We will be burying the dear fellow tomorrow morning. Triple grouse, please, Harry.'

'Er. Father Gorn. May I…'

Father Gorn cut Harry off once more, 'We wanted to bury him today as Julie said it was Paul's birthday, but we couldn't fit him in. Lot of deaths lately. Some sort of salmonella epidemic recently.'

A little sweat appeared on Jeff's brow. Father Gorn took a big gulp of his whiskey.

'Now, Father. I…' Harry got cut off again. 'Lovely weather for the time of year. Warm as punch. Makes for thirsty work.' The vicar drained the rest of the drink. 'Must get back to the church. Edna is giving bell ringing practice to the girl guides and I'm not sure she is showing them all the right moves. Thanks again for all you do. I know Julie was most grateful, when I saw her this morning. See you tomorrow.'

In Father Gorns head he is through the door before his body is, so little time he has. As he slipped out the front door, his robe caught on the corner of the fruit machine and three little miniature bottles of whiskey fell from a pocket, and land, unbroken, on the floor.

'He didn't want to pay for that drink, then.' Jeff complained.

'Or listen to what I had to say! Typical Suffolk skinflint. Looks like we're stuck with the stiff!'

Harry picked up a newspaper, rolled it up and put it under his arm. 'I'm just going to have a contemplate. I'll leave you with your mate for a minute or two!'

Jeff peered over at the coffin as Harry closed the door to the outside area. He slowly made his way over to the corner where the coffin stood. He felt a cold shiver go down his back as he reached it.

A Wedding and a Wake

Best remove those empty glasses. Can't do anything with those still on them. Jeff picked up a tray and placed all the offending glasses on it and took it to the bar. However, he was morbidly curious. What if Paul wasn't in there? What if there had been a mistake and it was an empty coffin. Problem solved. The coffin could be used for firewood for the next month. Save a bit on the heating. It was easy. All Jeff had to do was check that he was in there.

Jeff had taken the five or so steps needed to get back to the coffin, when Harry walked back in. 'What are you up to?'

Jeff continued his slow walk up to the coffin. 'I'm just going to check that Paul is actually in there.'

Harry looked on in disbelief, 'Where do you think he is? Down the chippy getting some halibut?'

Jeff carried on, regardless. 'You never know with Julie.'

'True.' Harry decided his brother was

The Regulars

right. You never know with Julie. He sheepishly followed his brother over to the coffin, keeping a little distance.

Jeff slipped his fingers into the edge of the top of the lid. He pulled. 'It's heavy.' The lid came up a few inches and Jeff pushed his face forward, tentatively, to look inside.

'Well?' Harry whispered, in anticipation.

'Yeah. He's all there.'

'Good. How's he look?'

'Pale.' replied Jeff.

'Pale? He's Nigerian!'

'Is he?' News to Jeff.

'Yes. Julie's surname is Ombongo! Here. Let's have a look.'

Jeff raised the lid a bit higher so Harry could see in. 'Aah. He's got a little smile.'

Harry relaxed, slightly. 'Yes. First bit of peace he's had I years, I'd say. Think I'd rather croak it than spend another twenty years with Julie.'

Jeff spotted something, 'What are a set of golf clubs doing in here?'

'Julie said he loved golf,' Harry replied,

A Wedding and a Wake

'Played off a one handicap, according to Julie.'

'That's better than Tiger Woods!' Jeff stated, 'Look, there's a pool cue too. And a set of darts. What is this? A jumble sale?'

Harry laughed, 'Either that or Julie's been clearing out the loft again! Right. He's in there, that's for sure. Close up. I've had an idea.'

Jeff put the lid down and gave it a good bang to make sure it was closed. 'What's this idea, then?'

Harry gave a knowing smile, 'We take him up the hall with us.'

'Yeah. He'd look good, propped up against the bar. Happiest day of their lives and we'd be saying to the guests 'Here's your drink, just mind the stiff in the corner!"

'Don't be an idiot. We take him up there now. Stick him under the stage, we'll then do the bar until the evenings over and then pull him out in the morning.' Harry certainly had a plan.

The Regulars

'Yeah that's not a bad idea. I thought you said I was doing the bar, here in the pub tonight?'

'Change of plan. I'll see if big Cliff can mind the pub for an evening.'

'Cliff will be at the wedding.' Jeff replied, 'You'd need to get someone in who is not invited.'

'Good point, Jeff.' Harry said as he tidied away some glasses. 'I could ask Cobweb Mary to do it. Just for a night. Not like there's going to be many people in here, if they're all up the hall.'

'If that's the only person left then all well and good. If she'll do it.'

'I'll ring her now. You find something to put over the coffin, so people don't see what we're doing. Don't want the village to think we're a couple of graverobbers, do we?'

Harry went into the next room to use the telephone. Jeff looked around for something to place on the coffin. Ah. They'll do. He picked up two pairs of his old chef whites he was no longer using

A Wedding and a Wake

and positioned them carefully over the coffin.

Harry came back in, 'Mary's sorted. She'll open up at seven for us. Go and reverse your van up as close to the back door as you can.'

Harry spotted the crusty old chef whites after Jeff had gone outside. Sorry about the whiff, Paul, he thought to himself. Once Jeff had returned, they both grabbed an end, each.

'All set, Harry.'

'You ready, Jeff?'

'Yes, go for it.'

The pair then lifted the coffin from its stool. 'He's heavy.' Jeff wheezed. 'Must be all that sports gear.'

The boys start walking out the door, rather unsteadily, with the coffin, but the corner of it bashed the new fruit machine, which then sprang into life, bleeped, flashed madly, and then, promptly died.

'Spiffing!' Harry cried. 'Carry on. We've haven't got long before people will be up

The Regulars

the hall to start setting up.'

Harry was reversing out the door when he hit his head on a low beam. This was easier said than done. Jeff's hand slipped and he dropped his end slightly into a load of pub trophies, cracking some.

'Careful. Mind the pool trophies.' Harry warned a little late.

'Yes. Twenty-four carat plastic!' Jeff snapped.

'One of those is mine!' Harry complained.

The boys twisted their way, with the coffin and get it outside. They switch the coffin round and Jeff backed himself up, just inside the back of the van.

Harry looked up and spotted the Rolls Royce of Lord and Lady Braithwaite coming into the car park. What a time for them to arrive!

'Oh god, quick. Get right in there!'

Harry pushed the coffin in hard. Jeff didn't have a clue what was going on and hadn't pulled his hand away quick enough. Bang! It squashed his right hand

A Wedding and a Wake

fully. He let out a large scream!

The coffin was in about as far as it could go, now, but was still protruding about half a centimetre. The Braithwaite's exited their roller and walked up to Harry, still at the back of the van.

'Good afternoon. The good lady and I would like to take lunch at your establishment.' Lord Braithwaite's beard had since grown back after their last meeting. 'Well. You do Bernard!' added her ladyship. 'Give them another chance, dear.'

Harry had to concede that they were not open as he tried his best to pull the chef whites back over the coffin.

'Not open? But it's Saturday afternoon, Man.'

Harry had to think quickly. 'The chef's not here. He's… er… broken his hand.'

Jeff couldn't see who was there and started climbing back over the coffin. 'Who's that, Harry.'

Harry snapped closed the van doors, right on Jeff's head to drown him out.

The Regulars

'Yes. Freak cooking accident I'm afraid. Bowl of minestrone soup fell on it!'

Her ladyship was not amused. 'Pity it didn't fall on his head. Come on, Bernard. We'll go to the Rat's head.'

'But they don't do food.'

'Neither do these! Come on!'

The lord followed his wife back to the car but turned back to Harry as he was about to take huis seat. 'You need to get your act together, Publican. Or you'll soon be closed.'

Harry gritted his teeth as he waved them goodbye. Sooner than you think, you posh pair of ponces.

He then opened the door to the back of the van. 'Sorry about that, Bruv. Lord and Lady Muck arrived. Had to get rid of them.'

Jeff emerged holding his right hand. 'I think it's broken.'

'Oh, you'll be alright,' Harry tried to reassure him, 'Get that adult channel on tonight and your grip will be like a vice!'

Jeff was driving his van, one handed, up

Drubbin road, towards the community centre. It was only a two-minute drive.

'Drive easy, will you, Jeff. We don't want him flying out the back!'

As the van went around the corner at the top of the road, Billy 'of the Ocean', was walking along with his normal plastic bag of beers. He had an open can in one hand and was happily swigging away.

He spotted the van turning the corner, and the chef whites slipped from the top of the coffin, exposing it for him to see. He looked at the packaging on the can and then threw it down on the ground.

The van pulled up at the community centre, near the front doors. The car park was empty which was a good sign that no one else had arrived to set up.

Jeff entered and turned on the lights. In the lobby was a small trolly. 'Excellent. We'll use this. Be a lot easier.'

Jeff positioned the trolly at the rear of the van and the brothers pulled the coffin out onto is as conspicuously as they could, and wheeled him in. As they entered the main hall, they were halfway through, when the door closed back on them, knocking the coffin off the trolly. The pool cue had fallen out but luckily, that was it. The boys closed the lid and placed it back on the trolly.

'My hand's still killing me.' Jeff complained, as he repositioned the chef whites, once again.

'Right. Come on.' Harry snapped.

Jeff spotted the pool cue and booted it down the length of the hall. He'd had enough.

Harry pulled up. 'I was thinking we could put him under the stage. No one ever goes in there. Only the panto lot and they are hardly going to be here today. Be okay for the night.'

They then wheeled the coffin a bit further to the stage, when they suddenly heard a voice. 'Oh. God. Stand there in front of it!' Harry said, flustered.

Bruce Bennett, the hall cleaner, then walked up to them, holding the pool cue.

'Boys. You're a bit early, aren't you?' he enquired as he pulled his spectacles down from his forehead.

'Yes, as usual.' Harry replied, trying to sound efficient. 'You know us, Bruce. We like to do a professional job.'

'Just making sure we're all stocked up.' Jeff added.

Bruce was looking down at the floor. 'What's wrong with people nowadays? I'm used to picking up fag butts and bits of chewing gum, but not flippin' pool cues. You don't have to help with the tables, lads. That's not your job.'

'We don't mind lending a hand' Harry looked at Jeff, 'Do we?'

'Nor a broken one!' Jeff sulked.

Bruce nodded over to the coffin. 'That tablecloth has seen better days.'

Harry sighed, 'That's Barry for you. Always a cheapskate.'

'Tighter than a wheelnut!' Bruce replied, 'I'll help you with the tables.'

'No, it's okay. You don't have to.' Jeff stood a bit closer to the coffin in case

The Regulars

Bruce came any nearer.

'No. I insist!'

Harry and Jeff looked at each other. Harry said 'You stay here with this. We won't be long.'

He then went off with Bruce and started setting up the tables, while Jeff remained an onlooker.

Harry grabbed a chance to mumble something to Jeff. 'We'll wait until he's gone and then we'll shove it under the stage.'

Jeff nodded back, cautiously.

Harry and Bruce had just put out the last table when the main doors swung open.

A rotund man and his younger assistant waltzed in with a speaker under each arm.

Bruce remarked, 'Blimey. Everyone's early, today.'

'Wotcha, Mate.' The large man announced in a booming voice. 'We're just going to unload all the disco gear, now and setting it up. I'll be leaving but

John-Boy here, will be staying with the equipment. I'll be back about sevenish.'

Harry was upset. 'What? He's staying with the equipment until seven?'

The portly man whipped out a handkerchief, wiped the sweat from his top lip. 'Yeah. Couple of months ago we were supposed to be doing a gig in Tonmarket, when all the gear got nicked! All they left were the chairs we sit on and a Shane Ward CD. Come on John-Boy. Get this unloaded. I've got to be in Fitwell Ash in an hour!'

The Disco boys dropped the speakers and then head out to get more equipment. Bruce is still up the other end of the hall.

'There's only one thing for it now. You'll have to stay with the coffin.' Harry informed Jeff.

'Bloody hell, Harry' moaned Jeff back at him.

'It's the only thing we can do. Look, I'll put one of those clean tablecloths on it and it should be fine. I think that poor

The Regulars

sod, Paul's had enough of having your dirty old chef whites on him for one day.'

'But Harry…'

'I've left the pub open and I've got to sort Cobweb Mary out. If Julie finds out we've got the body of her loved one, doubling up as a wedding breakfast table, we're done for. We'll sling him under the stage any chance we get.'

The Disco was all set up and John Boy was sat on a fold up chair, arms crossed, staring at the disco equipment. Jeff was sat one metre away from the coffin. There was silence. Occasionally they caught each other's gaze and turned away, annoyed.

The hall was dimly lit, but busy. The wedding meal had been had, the speeches had been spoken and all the toasts had been toasted. Harry was behind the bar serving Brassie and Cliff.

A Wedding and a Wake

'Guinness for me, please, Harry.' Cliff requested, 'Put a depth charge in it. Lager for Brassie. Put two in his!'

'Coming up…'

Brassie placed himself on one of the bar stools, not intending to move from it for the rest of the night. 'What's up with Jeff? He's by the wedding cake. Dancing on his own.'

Harry placed Brassie's lager in front of him. 'What's wrong with that? It's a wedding.'

'Yeah. But he's been there an hour and a half. Shouldn't he be helping you?'

'I gave him the night off.' replied Harry as the two depth charges sunk to the bottom of Brassie's pint glass.

'He didn't go overboard dressing up, did he?' Cliff added.

'Here, boys. Just mind the bar for a minute.'

Harry left the bar and wandered over to Jeff, who was still staying close to the coffin, which was doubling up as a table. Jeff was dancing. Only Jeff was dancing.

The Regulars

'Why did you let them put the wedding cake on it?' moaned Harry.

Jeff continued dancing. 'Barry said so. Said it was the best place for photographs. It's not my wedding, Harry. I've been dancing on the same spot for nearly two hours now. I'm busting for a leak an' all.'

Harry looked around at the bar and the large queue that was now forming.

'You'll have to go on watch for a bit. So I can take a pee.'

'I can't. Everyone wants the bar. Er... Look. Here's an empty pint glass. Do it in that. I'll cover for you.'

Jeff snatched the glass, obviously at breaking point. Harry stood in front of him as Jeff filled up the glass.

A young girl, who had been playing close to the boys, came up to Harry and tried to peek past him. Harry clipped her over the head and smiled back at her annoyed face.

'Here. All done.' Jeff tried to hand the full glass to Harry. 'I can't take that back with me. No one would buy any more drinks. Just leave it on the table. Get rid later, when they've all gone. I've got to get back to the bar. Keep dancing, Brucie!'

Jeff shook his head and started dancing once more.

Harry arrived back at the bar, to be greeted by Brassie shoving a full pint into his hand. 'Here you are Harry. Get this down you. Good stuff, this.'

'Bloody hell, boys. I'm working.'

Cliff pushed another full pint towards Harry. 'I thought you'd be celebrating after what Julie did?'

Harry put the pint back down on the bar. 'What are you on about?'

'She told Brassie, here, she went and paid all your unpaid rent this afternoon.' replied Cliff.

Barry was slightly sozzled and appeared at the bar for another refreshment, 'I don't mind the bar staff getting legless. It wouldn't normally stop Jeff! It's a day of celebration!'

Harry realised that his perilous financial position had come to an end. 'I always said she was a wonderful woman, that Julie. Sod it! Let's CELEBRATE!!!'
The Bar roared and everyone helped themselves to drinks.

An hour later, the bar area was empty, save for a couple of strangers snogging in the corner.
Barry and Maureen were smooching on the dance floor, inside a circle made by some of the guests. Harry was completely blotto, by this time, and staggered out of the toilets towards the circle, trying to join in. However, everyone had linked hands and there was no way through. He then spotted Jeff by the cake and remembered the coffin. He ambled up to him, as steady as he could and put his pint down.

'Sorry Jeff. Didn't mean to leave you here all night!'

'Yes. You look very concerned! Look at the state of you!'

A Wedding and a Wake

'Well. Well. We had a bit of good news.' Harry got the words out okay. 'The rent's been paid!'

Jeff couldn't believe it. 'Really? How?' Harry was trying to straighten his waistcoat but was failing, 'Julie, apparently, with her inherit… inherit… inheritance!'

'So? We're saved?' Jeff was pleased. Harry picked up a pint from the table.

'Yes. It seems that way.'

'You had better take her on again, now.'

'I'll speak to her tomorrow. Until then… cheers!'

Harry took a big gulp at his pint glass and then released he had picked up the glass that Jeff had urinated in earlier. He immediately spat out a giant gob full which, unfortunately, drenched poor old Maureen as she was dancing past. Jeff had tried to take cover and in doing so had grabbed hold of the tablecloth, pulling the cloth and the wedding cake off and onto the floor, exposing the coffin.

The Regulars

Everything stopped.

Everyone staring at Maureen. Her once, sparkling white dress, now covered in yellow liquid.

Father Gorn cut a forlorn figure in the church graveyard, the following day. There were not many mourners at the burial. Nor had there been expected, following the previous day's events.

The regulars had all made it. Out of respect for Julie.

The pallbearers lowered the coffin into the ground as Father Gorn read out a few words. Jeff smirked as he spotted lots of beer glass rings on the coffin lid, and the corner, slightly dented from the fruit machine. Julie dropped a rose into the hole and moved away.

Cliff then walked up with Brassie and dropped in a gold tee.

Barry and Maureen shifted forward and dropped in a dart flight.

Maureen then moved back and gave Harry a look as if from the devil itself.

Barry moved her on. Harry's eyes followed her as she went. Jeff took one look at Harry and burst out laughing. Maureen had given him the biggest black eye he had ever seen!

MISTLETOE AND CRIME

For the first time in over ten years it had snowed before Christmas in Sandwich Green. The village was bathed in a blanket of light flakes and a little Robin redbreast landed on top of the post box near the village shop. It was certainly the time to be merry for the regulars of the Lazy Dog public house. For it had been an eventful Saturday night, preceding Christmas eve. The bar takings had been good, and a jolly night was had by all. But this was now the early morning after. Very early.

Click, clink, went the glass bottles on the milkman's float as he turned the corner into Drubbin road, where the Lazy Dog stood, glistening under the streetlights. The sun had not yet broken through the early morning cloud although the stark, white coated ground shone up to give the place an eery luminescence.

Hubert, the village milkman of some three decades, dropped off his milk bottles and cartons at each of the houses in the street. At every other house, he picked up a small envelope containing a reasonable monetary bonus; a token for his sterling work in the early hours of each day.

He thought he knew what to expect when he reached the pub. He slipped the envelope out from behind the small potted evergreen where he drops the milk off. There was some hope as the envelope was bigger than last years. Not by much, but it had instilled a slight feeling of warmth that he was grateful for.

Hubert poked his finger in one corner of the envelope and slid it across to break the seal and slipped out the contents. His face dropped, as did the envelope. 'And a Merry Christmas to you, too! Peasants!'

* * * *

The room was large and foreboding, still in semi darkness. A strange nasal breath of air filled the room in intervals of five seconds. A gap in the curtains had started to let the first rays of sunlight into the chamber where, emerging from under a duvet, was a slowly stirring Jeff.

The sunlight had caught Jeff's left eye, which had awoken him from his lager induced coma. His head was pounding. Harder than possibly at any time he and his brother had been incumbents at the Lazy Dog. His eyes widened slightly, and he then realised. This wasn't his bedroom. In fact, this wasn't even the pub. The current thunderstorm in his brain stopped him from freaking out and jumping up. Instead, he slowly and tentatively lifted the foreign duvet and peeked underneath. Suddenly, Jeff let out a silent scream and dropped the duvet immediately. He froze, his actions halted by the immediacy of not knowing what to do next. He was not alone.

The nasal breathing had become slightly fainter and from beneath the duvet appeared a sausage like digit, followed by four more. A massive yawn and stretch meant the visible hand was now attached to a huge clump of forearm-like pink meat. The duvet slipped further off the bed and only a last-ditch effort by Jeff kept it partly over the huge body that laid next to him. The stirring became greater and eventually the body rolled over towards Jeff until its nose was resting on Jeff's chin. The increasing sunlight now meant that Jeff could make out the features. It was none other than Claudette, Big Cliff's older sister. She is the spitting image of the big rugby player. This was not a conquest that Jeff would be proud of. He jerked his face away from the nose and then slowly tried to ease his way out of the bed. As he did so, he heard the faint ramblings downstairs of a familiar voice. It was Big Cliff. If he found him in here, then he was a gonner. He managed to supress the panic and slid himself expertly out of the bed as if he'd done it before. Upon standing, he realised that he was completely naked, aside from a pair of Elf tights that he must had acquired from someone the previous night. Looking around for an escape route, he realised there was only one available. The Window.

Downstairs, in his kitchen, big Cliff

was sat at breakfast table with a stubby bottle of beer on the go. His wife, Brenda, a big lady herself, was frying a couple of packets worth of back bacon. The window was open to let out the immense steam coming from the pan.

'So, a quiet night at the pub then. Love?' Brenda enquired.

'Yeah,' replied Cliff, 'they had the bowls lot in for their Christmas meal. They had Jeff pretending to be Father Christmas or something. He was off his face!'

'He's always off his face, that one.' Brenda said as she placed one of the packs worth of bacon between a foot-long baguette.

'Not like this. He was steaming, big time. He left early, though.'

'Probably knew he'd had enough, unlike you. Here, take this cuppa up to your sister.'

Jeff was trying to open, very slowly, the large, heavy curtains that adorned Claudette's bedroom. Very carefully, he pulled them back so he could slip through without letting any more light into the room that might wake her. He then heard a foot and the first stair. It was Cliff. He now had to increase his speed as another foot landed on a stair.

Cliff had reached the landing but had spilt a bit of tea into the saucer so had a quick slurp to get rid of any evidence before entering his spare bedroom, where his sister was enjoying a lay in after accompanying him to the pub do the previous night.

Jeff was pulling at the window latch, but the frost had caused it to stick.

Cliff gently turned the handle, 'Claudie, love. Cup of tea for you,' and entered the room. His face immediately filled with terror.

Claudette was sitting bolt upright, beaming a wide Christmas smile.

Cliff relaxed. 'Oh, it's okay. I thought that shelf was going to fall down.'

Jeff had made it outside the window just in the nick of time. The outside air was cold to his naked torso as he shimmied down the available drainpipe. His hands slipped and he dropped the last six feet into a holly bush. Gradually, he gained composure and rubbed himself down, being careful not to appear from behind the bush. His bare nipples were now apparent to the freezing temperatures and his already red nose had turned a darker shade of crimson. He took a tentative look from above the bush and glanced both ways. Now was his chance. The pub was only in the next road and it was still early. Not many people about, if any. Go! He then goose stepped his way from out of the bush, looking behind him as he went. As he glanced round. Bump! Straight into Father Gorn.

'Good morning, young Jeffrey. Merry Christmas.'

Jeff tried covering his naked torso with both his hands that were now a sort of blue colour. 'Er… Merry Christmas, Father. You're about, early, aren't you?'

The Regulars

Father Gorn then actually noticed that Jeff was naked, save for a pair of green, nearly see-through stretched tights.

'I could say the same about you,' he then glanced up at the window that Jeff had just made his exit from.

'Oh, don't worry,' smiled the vicar, 'that's the same escape route I use. Be seeing you.' With that he was off on his merry way.

Harry was up and about early, as was normal after a night of joviality in the main bar. The remaining fittings had to be reattached with the glue he kept behind the bar and Cobweb Mary would be in soon to collect the broken glass from the floor. As he collected the tube from the bar drawer, he heard the slow creak of the back door. Burglars? DI Russell in for a quick pounce? No, it was Jeff, trying to creep in unannounced.

'Where the hell have you been?' Harry shouted, 'and what on earth are you 'hardly' wearing?'

Mistletoe and Crime

Jeff was annoyed with himself as, apart from Father Gorn, he had managed to get back to the pub without being seen.

'Tights, Harry.'

'I can see that,' boomed Harry, 'but whose?'

Jeff, without knowing it, pulled them a bit further up his tummy. 'They're from last night's do. I was being festive, like you asked.'

Harry pulled the dangling light fitting closest to the bar straight them applied a little glue. 'Go and get dressed. I could do with your help, here. The decorations need to be put up!'

'We haven't got any decorations' replied Jeff, a little bemused.

Harry smiled, 'Didn't you ever watch Blue Peter? There's a load of bog roll out the back. I'm sure you can make some decorations out of that. Plus, there's plenty of green bottles laying around. Stick a few tealights in them and we'll be sorted.'

'Why don't we just buy some?' Jeff

protested, still adjusting his tights. 'The rent's been paid. Surely we can stretch to that?'

Harry had glued his thumb and forefinger together and was now trying to prise them apart. 'Because, my young apprentice. The rent was paid, supposedly, in gratitude for helping Julie out with the wake. If she ever gets wind that her loved one was used to prop up Baz and Maureen's wedding cake, we'll be in the shithouse again!'

'I take your point.' Jeff was fascinated by Harry's ongoing attempts to release his digits.

'Go and get dressed, for god's sake!' bellowed Harry as he noticed Jeff still stood in the bar.

Julie, the now widowed barmaid, trudged through the snow in Drubbin road, heading to the Lazy Dog for her first shift, following her period of bereavement. The boys had been more than fair with her regarding her time off

Mistletoe and Crime

and she had felt pleased that she had been able to help regarding the rent. Being behind the bar gave her the chance to talk to so many people and that is when she felt happiest. Not sure that the other people felt the same but that's how a good pub is run.

'Welcome back!' Harry greeted Julie, affectionately. 'How do you like the bar? We put a few decorations up. What do you think?'

Julie looked up and around at the obvious home-made decorations. They were pitiful. She didn't know whether to tell the truth or be honest. Ultimately, she though honesty was the best policy.

'Harry. They're shit!'

'Okay, Julie. Just be blunt.' Harry was disappointed. He and Jeff had been all afternoon dying the tissue paper with food dye. Unfortunately, Jeff's cupboards were rather poorly stocked with food dye and it transpired he only had one colour: Dark blue!

Jeff popped his head round the bar.

The Regulars

'Hi Julie. Good to have you back. What do you think?'

'The decorations are not to Julie's taste, Jeff.' Harry said as he took her coat from her. A simple gesture but not something he normally does.

'Jeff's going over to Farmer Nash's in a little while, to get a Turkey. We'd like to invite you over for Christmas dinner tomorrow.'

Julie was a little overwhelmed. 'Yes. Yes, I'd like that. Thanks.'

'I thought you were getting the Turkey?' Jeff asked, as he tried to get the top off the washing up liquid.

'I was going to. But I've decided I'm going to ask all our regulars over for lunch tomorrow, as well. As a thank you for the past eighteen months we've been here. I told Farmer Nash, you would be over at four, so you'll have to be a bit lively. Oh. And there will be ten of us, so you need to make sure you pick out a big one.'

Jeff rolled his eyes. 'Hang on a minute.

Ten of us? There aren't that many regulars!'

'Yes. Big Cliff and his wife Brenda are coming. I saw them last night. Oh, and he's got his sister staying with them so I said she could come, too.' Harry smiled back at Jeff. 'Off you trot!'

Jeff pottered off, mumbling as usual.

Nash house farm was on the edge of Sandwich Green, the opposite direction to the Rat's head, on the main road through the village. It was usually a four-minute walk for Jeff, but in this snow and with his wellingtons, you could double it.

Jeff trudged up to the front door of the farmhouse and tapped the knocker a couple of times. Behind the door he heard a groan and then a few chairs screeching on a tiled floor.

The door eventually opened and there appeared Mavis Nash, the farmer's wife. She was covered head to foot in flour.

'Oh. I've obviously caught you at a bad

time.' Jeff acknowledged.

'No. It's alright, dear. I've nearly done. You must be from the pub? Brian said you'd be coming.' Mavis sneezed and a cloud of flour was blown into the air in Jeff's direction.

'If it's not too much trouble?'

'Not at all. Do come in.'

Jeff entered the house and was immediately into a large kitchen. On the table were roughly fifty freshly made mince pies, of the quality Jeff could only dream about.

'Wow. They smell lovely. You'll have to give me your recipe.'

Mavis frowned. 'Oh no. Couldn't do that. It's a family secret.' She opened the oven door and removed another tray of about twenty more mince pies. 'You'll need to go find Brian out the back. He's in one of the shed's somewhere.'

Jeff remained in the kitchen for a bit, taking in the delightful baking smell and then took himself off out the back door.

The back yard was barely lit and only a

faint light could be seen at the back of the yard. Jeff decided to head for it.

As he walked through the snow, which had been mixed with muck, making each footstep a sticky one, echoes of cow calls, pigs grunting, and turkey's panicking, filled his eardrums.

Just then, Farmer Nash appeared in a shed door frame, holding a dead lamb in each hand, by the neck.

'Whas go'on 'en, buh?'

'I'm sorry?' Jeff replied, not understanding.

'Ah said, What's do'on wi yat?'

Jeff just stood there. Did he just ask how he was? Did he just tell him to go away? He had better reply. 'I'm from the pub… Come to pick up a turkey? For Christmas.'

Farmer Nash grunted and then motioned for Jeff to follow him. He took him to another shed that had a little more light going on inside. However, there was a problem. They had reached the turkey shed but they were all still alive. Running around.

'As there one's. You aren't a killin?'

Oh my god. Jeff still didn't understand. Did he expect him to kill one of the turkeys or was he going to do it?

'See'in ya, buh. Haz's noice Christmas.'

Problem solved. Nash had buggered off. Jeff had to do it himself!

It was Christmas morning in Sandwich Green, and the village had been coated in a light pattering of flakes making it look nice and clean. All except for a set of mucky footprints leading back to the pub.

Inside the main bar, Harry had pushed the tables together to create enough room for a sitting of ten to eat together. He then placed all the knives and forks out as Jeff came in from upstairs.

'Morning Harry. Merry Christmas.' Jeff placed a wrapped present, resplendent with a little bow in front of him.

'Ah thank you, Jeff. Merry Christmas to you too.' He picked up the present, 'You shouldn't have. Can I open it now?'

'Be my guest.' replied Jeff.

Harry started pulling some of the wrapping tape away. 'Say, you made a bit of a racket when you came in last night.'

Jeff replied, 'Yeah. I brought a bird home.'

'Well done, my son. You'll be in a good mood today then.'

Harry released the gift from the wrapping and found that Jeff had got him a Christmas themed waistcoat.

'I like this. Thank you, Bro. I'll wear it today.' Harry then walked over to the bar and produced his present to Jeff.

'Ah you got one this year!' Jeff was surprised. 'You don't normally go a lot on Christmas.'

'Well. Flash came in the other night and I'd had a few.'

'Oh god. This isn't something Flash sold you?' Jeff's tone had changed. 'Bound to be a scarf lead or something.' He tore the corner for little peak and saw a flash of red cloth. 'Well it's not a scarf

The Regulars

lead…' He then tore a bit more and revealed a bow tie. 'Oh. That's unusual.'

Harry laughed, 'It's a Christmas bow tie. See, it lights up in the middle and the other bits spin round when you press that button.'

Jeff tried to look grateful, 'You go this off Flash, did you? Bit bright for him?'

'Oh, he's got one as well. He'll be wearing it today.' Said Harry, 'Say, could you do the dinner for about three? I've asked them all to be here for two so we can have drinks and that, first.'

'Dinner? Oh yes. Of course. Three P.M.'

Harry opened a bottle of sherry and poured out two small glasses. 'Cheers.'

Jeff drank his in one go. 'Harry. There's something I need to tell you.'

Harry had only taken a small sip. 'yes?'

'Well you know the turkey you sent me to get?'

Harry put the glass down. His festive mood appeared to change. 'You didn't get it?'

'No. I got it alright. Just there's a small problem.'

'What?'

'It's not dead, yet!'

Harry burst out laughing. 'You're joking, Jeff?'

'Well you know that bird I said I brought home. That was the turkey.'

'You brought it back still alive?'

'Yeah. It's not my fault, Harry. I couldn't understand a word that farmer said, and he just left me there with the birds! I didn't know what to do?'

Harry shook his head then stopped, looking upwards, 'Where is it?'

Jeff shirked, 'It's in my room…'

Harry tentatively turned the handle to Jeff's room and pushed the door forward. He was immediately hit in the face with a bunch of turkey feathers. He spat them out and pushed the door open further. The room was a tip. The turkey had trashed the room. There were feathers and mess everywhere, but no

The Regulars

turkey.

'Look at the state of this room!' bellowed Harry. Jeff popped his head in. 'It normally looks like that. Minus the feathers and turkey crap.'

'Where's the bird?'

'It's in there somewhere. Look harder.'

'You look harder. I'm not going in there. It's your room!'

Jeff stepped forward into the room, looked around for a few moments before announcing, 'It's not here.'

'I can see that. Where is it then?'

'It was here when I came down. I gave it some water.'

Harry was perplexed, 'We'll have to search the pub. You'll never get it cooked in time now.'

Jeff came out of his room and closed the door. Harry checked his own room before checking the rest of the upstairs. Jeff had gone downstairs and was checking the kitchen and pool table side of the pub. The boys were turkey-less!!

All the regulars were taking their seats

at the table in the pub. Newlyweds Barry and Maureen were sat opposite each other. Big Cliff and his wife, Brenda were sat opposite each other with Cliff's sister, Claudette taking up two spaces towards the end. Julie was sat next to Harry, with a spare seat next to Flash.

Jeff had just brought in a bowl of vegetables and placed it on the table when he spotted that the only two seats left were either next to Flash, or the one next to Claudette. He went back into the kitchen to get the meat. Could he face a Christmas dinner having a conversation with Flash or could he sit next to Claudette, hoping she might have been so sloshed she wouldn't remember their little dalliance? He chose the latter.

Jeff brought the meat dish in and placed it on the table, 'I'm afraid we haven't got turkey this year. So, I'm hoping you will enjoy this.'

Barry inhaled a whiff of freshly cooked meat. 'Mmmm. Smells nice, Jeff.'

There were nods of agreement all round

as Jeff sat down next to Claudette.

Harry stood up and said grace and then everyone tucked in. Cliff was halfway through his mains when he gestured over to Jeff, 'You not having the meat, Jeff?'

'No, Cliff. I'm going vegan for new year.'

'Doesn't mean you can't have any now, does it?'

Jeff felt a large hand clutch his inner thigh as Claudette leaned over and whispered in his ear, 'You can have all the fresh meat you want; you know…'

Jeff squirmed and replied to Cliff, 'Just thought I'd start today, that's all.'

Within half an hour, everyone had finished. 'Would you like dessert now or shall I leave it for a bit.' Jeff enquired.

'Couldn't eat another thing.' Barry exclaimed.

'Leave it a while.' Said Cliff.

'That was scrumptious. Thank you, Jeff.' Maureen added.

'I didn't know you had it in you, Jeff.' Harry stated. 'Tell me. What exactly was the meat?'

There was then a knock at the door.

'Someone trying for a Christmas pint I expect?' Harry got up out of his chair, 'I bet this is Billy 'of the Ocean'. He's a chancer even though he's banned.'

Harry opened to door to reveal DI Russell.

'Merry Christmas, Knocker.'

'How do, Detective Inspector. Merry Christmas to you. Um. Anything I can do for you?'

'I've just had a call from your neighbour, Mrs Goodrum, my Mum. It appears her cat has gone missing… sometime this morning!'

'Oh? Really. It normally lays on the ledge of the pub kitchen window. Say, Jeff. You wouldn't know anything about it, would you?'

Jeff had gone a shade whiter than a whiter shader of pale. They'd all just eaten it!

Merry Christmas!!

The Regulars

ABOUT THIS BOOK

The seeds of the 'Regulars' was dreamt up one night at the Ipswich Regent while waiting for Ultravox to take the stage. Unfortunately, I'd mistakenly got my brother, Paul, there an hour early. Whilst staring at the empty stage we got to talking about the fact that we ought to write a stage show or sitcom. We settled on a pub setting. The following week Paul had knocked up a first draft of a sitcom script which had a lot of the characters fully formed. Over the course of the next three to four months we had managed to put six scripts down on paper. We then put them to one side and there they sat for the next three years. Until we had the crazy idea of filming an episode ourselves. The episode we chose to film was 'Bed, Breakfast and Beer' and is available on youtube with us both making an appearance. Paul's appearance larger than mine in many respects!